BAD LIGHT

BAD LIGHT

CARLOS CASTÁN

Translated from the Spanish by
Michael McDevitt

HB Hispabooks Publishing

Hispabooks Publishing, S. L.
Madrid, Spain
www.hispabooks.com

Originally published in Spain as *La mala luz* by Ediciones Destino, 2013
First published in English by Hispabooks, 2016
English translation copyright © by Mike McDevitt
Copy-editing by Cecilia Ross
Design and photography © simonpates - www.patesy.com

ISBN 978-84-943658-5-0 (trade paperback)
ISBN 978-84-943658-6-7 (ebook)
Legal Deposit: M-156-2016

**With the support of the
Creative Europe programme
of the European Union**

The European Commission support for the production of this publication
does not constitute an endorsement of the contents which reflects the views
only of the authors, and the Commission cannot be held responsible for any
use which may be made of the information contained therein.

For V.

CONTENTS

"I could just remember how my father used to say that the reason for living was to get ready to stay dead a long time."

W. FAULKNER, *As I Lay Dying*

"We were dead and we could breathe."

PAUL CELAN, "Memory of France"
Sand from the Urns

"To explain with words from this world that a ship parted from me with me on board."

ALEJANDRA PIZARNIK, *Tree of Diana,* 13

I. THE MONSTER

"The monster was made by fear."

William Lindsay Gresham,
Nightmare Alley

1

(dead behind these eyes)

The two of us had recently moved to Zaragoza, in the space of a few short months, Jacobo first, then me, both newly separated, still bearing the imprint of a wedding band on our fingers, that ring of slightly paler flesh that serves as a sort of badge, announcing one's newly unveiled, somewhat shameful solitude to the world. I guess we were each on the run in our own way. He, intent on starting afresh after his early retirement, and I perhaps somehow following in his footsteps, not so much out of relief at being able to call on his company from time to time as having been seduced, I believe, by the powerful lure that beginnings have always held for me, the blank page, starting over anew, any situation that can in my mind's eye conjure up ships burning in distant bays or homes left behind without prior warning, just like that, without turning the key in the lock, leaving on the table the dirty dishes from the evening meal the night before. People, say, who are released from jail or discharged at last from the hospital after a harrowing detox and who, with a handful of belongings, rent out a room in some unknown place, far from everything that happened before, placing their toothbrush in a glass on the sink, tossing a couple of changes of clothing into the drawers, and perhaps also a revolver or a photograph of a woman in a picture frame that can barely stand upright, before opening the window to air out the room and let the show commence. Then they see the neon lights on the building across the street and the hustle and bustle of a hostile neighborhood in which they'll gradually have to get their bearings. An official secondment at the right time or the taking up of a new administrative post can offer something along similar lines, the feeling of being alive against all odds and of the blank page still smelling of the printing press, awaiting events and ink. And all this despite the weariness and the old chains they will no doubt still have to drag behind them, shackled to their feet.

When Jacobo told me the details of his move and the opening measures of what appeared to all intents and purposes to be a proper new life, I couldn't help but feel, if we're calling a spade a spade, a twinge of envy, for one tends, if only intermittently, to feel, out of an instinct for survival, that there is time yet to endow our remaining days with some sort of meaning and to build a new tower in the middle of nowhere so as to carry on living—a longing, in short, for a change of scene, for new faces, for the simple possibility of losing my way down streets that lead who knows quite where or grabbing a coffee in bars in which I had never before set foot, a city, when all is said and done, with its mean streets and movie theaters, its record stores, its bookshops, its nights so similar to real nights. Everything as if to scale, like a toy, but real at the end of the day and waiting around the next corner. In the small town we first called home (for so many years, and how long each and every one of them felt), the lovely Provincia, it's as if the fog of tedium—which of its own accord, as a matter of course, already cloaked the evenings after a certain hour, steeping our bones in the dampness of a life already lived, a festering, repeated sorrow, like a strange morning dew, a sort of backward sweat that penetrated, from the outside in, the pores of every wall and of all that had gone before and was to come, leaving them drenched in emptiness and past and an ancient weariness that condemned you to walk half-slouched, to read listlessly, to endless naps so as not to have to see the pitiful death throes of time beneath the bad light that as soon took possession of the streets as it did the insides of homes and bars—had slowly been thickening.

We had met years before, Jacobo and I. For quite some time, we would see one another almost every day, the standard, more or less routine after-work beer, lingering a little longer with each passing evening, sometimes until the early hours. That getting to know one another started out as something ecstatic and life affirming. There were not enough days in the week to see through all the plans we hatched, or hours in the night to list them. Such affinities are above all else a matter of focus, a way of looking at the world; all of a sudden you find someone who not only places the source of light in the exact same spot as you, they also train it in precisely the direction you were looking. Many people decide to take their leave from this world one way or another, but it is not often that two people do so at the same time and through the same door, seeing everything from then on from a very distant, identical angle. When such a coincidence does arise, it's possible to scorn and admire in unison all that the world around us sets before our eyes, and to laugh at things, above all things held semi-sacred by the rest of humanity, untouchable subjects, delicate matters that cease to be delicate in the wee small hours, as if by magic after a certain time of night, amid the smoke of bars where customers stagger in and out under the weight of their histories, shadows in raincoats who drift across our field of vision and order drinks they down alone while the music devours them, characters in a theater too small to be taken all that seriously. Above all else, Jacobo liked to talk of women, both his more remote girlfriends (too many for my battered memory to retain the circumstances and names of with the precision he would have liked from his conversation partner, so as not to have to go over the same ground again and again) and his more recent extramarital conquests. His chatter could slide into an alarming muddle of dreamy girls and lion-like women, of more or less true exploits and others that amounted to little more than intentions or plans not fully thought through, a veritable verbal maze of flesh and fantasy in which I quickly got lost amidst all the many female names being mentioned, all the letters being sent back and forth, all the panties being hoisted up and yanked down. Never before, not even in movies, had women struck me as being as desirable as when recounted by Jacobo, nor amorous exploits as unsettling as when told in his words. His lips glistened as he recalled bedrooms, and skirts raised in the most precarious of hiding places, bare feet doing their sweet work beneath the most formal dining tables, some tales from way back, other from four days previously, surrenders and fits of madness, candor and fury, his arms catching the faintings of what seemed like ladies of myth suddenly transformed, as if by dint of a magical kiss, into mere broads, disheveled and stunning, panting and filthy. At first I feared that, as was only fair, he would expect similar confessions on my part, with the same degree of salaciousness and detail, but he soon realized I was far from comfortable discussing these matters, even at such times as those, when glasses are emptied quickly and I know the whole world is sleeping.

In contrast to that sort of never-ending revelry, the flip-side of the brandy and the music, was what had from an early age been his life's obsession: the horror of the German concentration camps and all their offshoots. His father had been a survivor of the Mauthausen camp, and he spent the years that followed his release tirelessly delivering seminars and all manner of speeches on his experience, on the duty to remember, and on his strange sense of guilt at having emerged alive from a hell in which so many had perished in the flames. Much like Primo Levi, he came to understand that public opinion eventually grows weary of a message repeated a thousand times over, he discovered that the world no longer wished to hear that tale of atrocity, especially after the start of the Vietnam War, which, as if it were a new, exuberant fad, rendered all that had to do with the previous barbarity outmoded in a matter of days. The image of horror was now that of napalm setting the jungle alight and no longer that of naked corpses piled up on the snow. Overnight, the World War was old news, as were the walking skeletons, the wheelbarrows full of carcasses with faces, the forced labor, the incinerating rooms, and the gas chambers. And also like Primo Levi, he ended his days by throwing himself headlong down a stairwell, weary of empty lecture halls, of deaf ears, and of the dreadful echoes of his own silence. The legacy handed down to Jacobo by his father was, above all else, guilt. He found it hard to forgive himself for not having listened more and better when the time came, for having, from a young age, grown bored without bothering to feign interest in the same old stories that tended to lead to the same tear-drenched scene, which struck him as being just as pathetic as it was unbearable. One always grows weary of other people's nightmares and of the late-night screams from the room next door, no matter who those screams come from. You can listen for a while, take their hand in yours, stay up all night, offer a sedative, a glass of water, but if what you truly want is to carry on living, you have no choice but to mount some sort of barricade against all that, to turn a deaf ear, and, one way or another, to distance yourself. To beat a retreat, leaving the one who's screaming on their own. It's like abandoning a wounded man in a ditch at a moment when the enemy is advancing at breakneck speed and it would be foolhardy to stay put and watch him bleed to death. Only after his father's death did Jacobo take any real interest in the story told by that broken man who wept at the movies, even the most lighthearted, screwball comedies, who sank into the couch, who sometimes came to a halt, gaze lost in the distance, the soup spoon hovering midway between the bowl and his lips. Jacobo read everything he could find on the subject, did his best to spread the word, and tried to take possession of that vision of horror. He felt he owed his father the nightmares that followed, the sleepless nights, the fears, the shadowy executioners roaming all night long through rooms and hallways. I'd even say that in some strange way he grew to love that inherited suffering that, amid horror in spades, gave him back something of a father's tenderness, a certain scent of home, the perfume of the old, bearable, just punishments. There are those who hoard, as if their lives depended on it, the pocket watch of a loved one, a portrait, an old fountain pen, or a lock of hair by way of a memento; Jacobo, meanwhile, had that fear. And he tended to it in his own way, he nourished it with photographs and memories and books. At first, when he spoke to me of the matter, I would feel somewhat uneasy and lower my gaze without knowing how to react, much like when as a child you have to offer your condolences to a classmate who's buried his mother two days previously. You're never sure whether it is best to meet the tragedy with silence or words, whether to embrace the person, offer them your sandwich, or simply leave them be. Jacobo, however, as if he had taken the lesson to heart, took pains not to endow the matter with any particular gravitas in our conversations. He preferred to dwell on more or less general questions that interested him, such as how humans react when pushed to a breaking point, survival, endurance, the power of a grudge. And it was astonishing how easily we skipped from that subject to others in our conversations; without realizing it, we'd again be discussing the idle gossip of the world around us, music and women, the trips we'd make one day, and all of the cards yet to be played.

All things considered, I think that in the end we never managed to be good for one another. Without wishing to, we dragged each other down into our respective pits, each drawn by the other's darkness and the force of his eddies. We never truly knew how to help one another with what really mattered, instead we behaved like that pair of men drowning in the sea who, as they go under, cling so fiercely to their saviors, with arms and fingernails, that they end up dragging them down with them to the depths. Without saying a word, as if by instinct, we stopped seeing one another with such frequency, and tedium once again descended. This is how things stood in the months leading up to my departure from home, and so things remained thereafter, in the days of the apartment rented out in great haste, the brutal solitude, the lowered blinds, and the doors locked night and day, as if all those precautions served any purpose and shadows couldn't pass through walls and pores.

2

(life back then)

And that, more or less, was what life back then was like,
before the move. Frozen, deserted streets, a newly rented
apartment with someone else's furniture, silence, hours
spent beneath the naked bulb on the living room ceiling,
the pointlessness that seemed to have come to rest on
things, slowly, much as a layer of dust forms without our
noticing, taking possession of them, cloaking everything
in a sort of grimy, drab gauze. That's what the days of my
life were like back then. The evenings at home, stunned. I
sometimes sit down at the table to eat, without the slightest
hunger. I am my own mother; I am, at one and the same
time, the downcast young boy and the voice that tells him
to try and cheer up, to pull himself together already, to look
after himself, to swallow, even if he doesn't feel like it, a
few spoonfuls of rice, one more, you'll feel better, you'll
see, I'll feel better, I'll see. I remember the fear I once
was, made flesh, a bundle of nerves, and how I sensed my
own presence much as one might perceive a tremor, the
juddering of a worn-out heart that seemed to be shifting

position constantly inside its chest, without ever finding the right spot. I see myself seated in the armchair next to the glass door that looks onto the balcony, wearing a coat buttoned up to my neck. I'm not sure if I can't move or don't want to. It's hard to say; I don't move, that's all. I give a start at the slightest noise from the street or the stairway, the buzzing of the intercom whenever it's pressed over and over again by the mailman or the junk mail distributors. And I remember the dread at the thought of losing my mind, of being unable to return, and also the odd snatch of the disjointed ramblings running through my thoughts, shot through with static and barking and stinging music and hazy questions—who took me away, and where to, I cannot sense myself here, in this voice that's apt to start talking alone in the middle of the evening, uttering the names of people long gone, or in the hand that, almost without realizing it, scribbles these marks in delirious ink (words in the universal and equally baffling language of the shakes) that cannot be deciphered later, nor can I spot myself in these wretched lines that seek me out, that enquire nervously on the pages of a notebook after my wellbeing, my whereabouts, what I could possibly be up to at this hour, and where in God's world and down what roads. And while I know that I am both the escaped prisoner running nonstop on wounded feet and the search party, armed to the teeth, that's hunting me down and setting the pack of hounds on my trail, I do not recognize as my own the footsteps looking for me in damp hotels, and ports, down solitary streets, in unmade beds, in secluded bars (of the sort you only ever visit once, of the sort never to be found again, as if, on your departure, they sank into a fog that is not of this world). Nor do I see myself in the anguish calling out to me because it's getting late and I'm nowhere to be seen, shouting a name that's mine, or at least it once was. It calls the name out louder and louder, with a voice increasingly hoarse, until it is little more than a straight-out moan, roaming the passageways of the labyrinth, the banks of the swamp, the forests of the night—the wailing of a monster that remembers me.

The telephone rings sometimes, not too often. Some calls I leave unanswered, I'm simply incapable of responding. Talking strikes me as a task as impossible as it is meaningless. Sometimes I do pick up the handset, silently praying it's nothing, a wrong number, and that no one is really looking for me or wants anything of me. I'm afraid of what the voice, whoever it may be, might summon up from the other end of the line, of the people it might name and of the memories all those words might unearth. I'm afraid of being made to cry. There are no friendly voices now. They do not exist, nor can I conceive of them. There is no such thing right now. In one way or another, they all link directly to the world, to the anxious, insufferable drone the world has become on the other side of the window. I peer out every now and again. There is usually nothing more than a frozen void through which a car passes once in a while. The shades of gray change depending on the time of day. The worst of them coincides with the hour when all activity appears to have died down and yet it's not altogether late. The stores are still open, lights can be seen in some windows, and silhouettes cast by people starting to lay the table, the clatter of dishes and cutlery; on the sidewalk across the street, a young boy is making his way home from some after-school class, a book bag on his back. Out there, where all that can now be seen is this gloomy, wind-battered watercolor, is where my life was until recently, a life from which I have stumbled like an elderly man on an ice-covered path. I've landed on the skull and crossbones, I don't remember how many turns I have to skip before I can rejoin the game.

I get snagged on words. There are those that take root somewhere in the brain and, despite my best efforts, refuse to budge. I think of the word *home* while the radio relays news of the Siberian cold front that swept through the country overnight, while I tossed and turned in bed, in search of a position in which sleep would come—mountain passes closed, school classes canceled in some northern cities due to snow, warnings not to use the car save in cases of dire need. I ponder that expression, *dire need*, and I'm on the verge of tears again. Home is a child in pajamas racing down a hallway, his bedtime long since passed, and also the voice from the kitchen telling him not to go around barefoot or he'll catch a cold, to drink up his milk, and to get into bed already. A bed with four little corners, a picture book on the bedside table. Dire need. Fear all of a sudden of the tenderness such an image conjures up. Panic, in truth, for I know that even in all its foolish simplicity, when tenderness strikes, it takes no prisoners; I don't know what the hell kind of strings get tugged at with the mere sight of an abandoned toy in the corner, a colored pencil that turns up out of the blue where you least expect it, a sticker album card with some soccer player on it that emerges, covered in fluff, when sweeping under the bed. I don't know what incendiary buttons all this pushes. Dire need—a soft cheek when the time comes to say goodnight, the raspberry toothpaste scent that enveloped that kiss now gone, never to return. On my afternoon stroll, at the new releases table, I paused to leaf through an album showcasing much of the work of the photographer Lewis Hine. Lying in wait on one of its pages, opened at random, was an image I was unable at that moment to endure (this often happens to me, I look at many things I should not): a young boy, a roving newspaper vendor in the years of America's Great Depression, has fallen asleep, utterly spent, on the stoop of a building. He's sitting on one of the steps, his head resting on a pile of unsold newspapers he's placed a few stairs up as a pillow. There is nothing more dramatic in the photo than a young boy overcome by tiredness and hiding from his employer's eyes in an attempt to replenish some of the strength he's used up hawking papers in those neighborhoods of cracked sidewalks, at bus stops, and out in front of office blocks. The photo reveals no injuries or any trace of tears or torture. None of that was necessary for me to know for certain, at that moment, as I contemplated that snapshot, that if, by some twist of fate, that boy had been one of my own children, I would be unable to spend a single moment of my remaining days doing anything other than hurling rocks through windows, setting off bombs left, right, and center, assassinating chancellors, burning down palaces, until I was gunned down by a well-aimed shot from a crack sniper crouching behind the open door of a patrol car. The upshot of this bewildering mess of memories and ideas that act as if they had a life of their own and come to land on my brain like crows is that the things for which I'd lay down my life are things I no longer have. I've either lost them or I've lost myself, but either way, I reach out and touch nothing but thin air.

The radio says that the blizzard now battering my windowpanes swept through Moscow some twenty hours ago. It arrived at my door after turning the domes of the Kremlin white and sweeping through nighttime Europe, steam rising from millions of boilers working at full blast while men and women sleep. It's mighty cold in this part of the planet. Save under this heap of blankets, where I lie motionless in a fetal position, all is night and frost, icicles hanging from eaves, water turning to ice in the pipes, whole litters frozen solid in their dens. Out there, everything hisses, everything roars.

It is all but impossible to keep the anguish at bay when it comes with a convoy of memories en masse, jumbled together, like a slew of arrows unleashed at once without taking proper aim, to see which one might pierce some flesh off in the distance, which one might tear through a nerve, which one might burst open an eye. In my dreams I am hunted by hounds and torches, my first name, my last name, called out endlessly, while I crouch shivering in the bushes, trying to keep my breathing in check, to keep stock still, to keep from coughing. I often wake up in the middle of the night, not always able to recall what I was dreaming when I sit bolt upright. I then have to get out of bed, switch on a lamp or two, rinse my face. My heart still racing. It only knows how to work toward one goal, the poor thing, and in its determination to pull in the direction of my survival, regardless of whether that's reasonable or otherwise, it allies itself with the storms. It pumps blood nonstop, unable to do anything else, sending it to the farthest vessels, to the tips of my fingers and toes, to my trembling brain, and this is tantamount to fueling the endless flow of images through my mind, words and ghosts, memories roaming in packs, the faces of those I miss the most, some of whom have already left this world for good and others I wish had done so a long time ago, eyes that once looked on me with love. There are momentary truces every now and then, but there is nothing so fragile and slippery as that deceptive calm. Occasional buffers against the disquiet sometimes occur to me, hideouts that, no sooner have I tried them out, prove utterly ineffectual. In search of refuge, my natural proclivities lead me back to the books that in times gone by, in previous slumps, in now half-forgotten debacles, succeeded in restoring me to the land of the living. But my concentration span is now all but nonexistent. I have no use, therefore, for full-length stories in which to immerse myself, since they all spit me out whether I like it or not, but rather, if anything, an atmosphere, a mood, some piece of prose that's halfway fit to live in, any context-free passage that might fleetingly conjure the illusion that I'm shaking off the sorrow into which my feet sink as I try to walk and managing, at least in part, to wrench free of myself. I seek in words an old familiarity, a homely air, so to speak, a warmth that, though it ultimately always proves ephemeral and elusive, achieves the momentary illusion of a temporary ceasefire in the midst of the never-ending battle my nerves are waging against themselves. Holding the remote, I look for channels showing classic movies or, at least, movies released in Spain no later than the seventies, just to hear the voiceover artists of the time. The sound is one I find particularly heartwarming. No matter what words come out of those lips that never appeared on screen and must now be dead, they take me back to my grandmother's living room, to the stale chocolate and the can of condensed milk, to the cookies snatched without permission from an aluminum tin in the pantry, the drowsiness after Sunday dinner with the specter of Monday already lurking on the other side of a few hours of restless sleep, a green, imitation-leather couch coming apart at the seams, and the shootouts in black-and-white taking me gloriously out of the world, the sweet talk, the skyscrapers, the blondes, the car chases.

3

(getting back home)

That was around the time of the spectacular accident in the Chilean mine. Thirty-three workers trapped almost half a mile beneath the earth. In real time, heart in mouth, the world followed the tragic events that, for seventy days, TV news bulletins the length and breadth of the planet led with. As did the press, and the radio. It was practically the only talking point. First, a tunnel was opened up through which the rescue teams could introduce the medicines and provisions from the outside world that were deemed most urgent. Direct, fluid communication was then established with those trapped below, their fears probed, their hopes of making it out alive broadcast, their attempts to say farewell in the darkest hours, their messages of love, their ham-handed poetry, filled with a candor that was chilling in its simplicity—pure naïf horror. People wondered what it might feel like to be trapped beneath a hillside, with tons of earth above and all that uncertainty as to whether one might ever again see the sunlight and all that it normally bathes. Little by little we learned of each individual case, the names and circumstances of the miners imprisoned down there below, hell almost within touching distance. The images on TV revealed the desperation of the relatives who followed operations as closely as they were allowed, night and day pressed up against the wire fence that marked the security perimeter. Both inside and outside the collapsed underground passageway, the slogan the whole world clung to was "get back home". Like the wounded soldiers in Vietnam field hospitals who, in their fevered state, dreamt of streetlights on a Saturday night, the smell of hamburgers, and of music, and of sex. Getting back home.

I felt sure that those thirty-odd men must include at least one who, after the obligatory homecoming in front of the cameras and the official celebrations, having shaken off the hordes of dignitaries and special correspondents, the well-wishers, the throng of microphones thrust before him, would return home alone to find everything precisely as he had left it, a glass of water filled with specks of dust on the bedside table, in the exact same spot he had placed it, no doubt a dirty dish with the remains of a meal from over two months before on the kitchen table, now infested with mold and ants. Everything precisely as it had been when he left for work that morning, the blinds lowered to the same height, the half-open doors, the unmade bed, a towel on the bathroom floor. I couldn't help but identify with that miner who, on his return, no sooner having set foot in the door, would be engulfed by the silence of his own home, a couple of dingy rooms in, say, the city of Copiapó. I wondered what would have gone through his mind those two long months buried down there below, while the others spoke of getting back

home, of almost Christmassy scenes, and of the collective
desire to make up for lost time if they ever made it out
alive, of what truly matters: the fair, ponies, Sunday picnics
in the country with the whole family, a hearty barbecue,
everyone helping to wash the car in the stream; no more
pisco ever again, no more anything ever again, just tucking
the children in to sleep, taking them for a Sunday stroll to
El Pretil or Schneider Park, thanking God for each new
morning, each breath of fresh air, and the light, above all
the light, enjoying whatever scarcity, whatever abundance.
He would dream, perhaps, that some former girlfriend had
heard news of his confinement, or some old friend from
his school days he cannot now recall, but who knows, or
some former drinking buddy, waiting for him up there
on the surface of oxygen and stars to crack open a bottle
in celebration. He would lie to his fellow inmates, telling
them that someone was waiting for him, that whether he
lived or died was not entirely inconsequential, that someone
somewhere cared about the fate that awaited his bone-dry,
malnourished hide all flecked with dirt and copper dust.
I thought of him at night, of that Chilean brother. He
appeared to me in dreams more than once, and we waxed
shyly philosophical in short phrases and lengthy silences,
much as certain wise men do when the day is done, by the
fireside, and all the cattle have been rounded up in their
pens. Life goes on as long as someone is waiting for you,
the rest is just survival, he would say, though survival plain
and simple is not without its charm and its thrills. Although
I knew it was a copper rather than a coal mine, he would
always appear with his face blackened, like a guerilla
readying an ambush in the darkness of the jungle. I also

31

always pictured him with filthy hands and black fingernails. I'm not sure he was right, my Chilean brother, about the waiting and the survival, but I grew somewhat fond of that coal-stained shadow who smoked while gazing at the floor and swigging bitter *mate* in my dreams.

Contrary to what tended to happen to me, the affliction I experienced at that time was a sorrow that emerged almost wordlessly, a naked ache that couldn't find the right expression, something akin to an animal-like tearing, with all its bafflement and its momentous howl, like a dog waking up from the anesthesia under which its kidney has been clumsily extracted. In my mind, only objects, pure and simple, as if their sheen of connotation or memory had been wiped clean, the boredom of passersby on the other side of the window. It's a liquid ache that drenches language, that deluges all thought like a dirty wave, dissolving concepts, soaking my knot of cables and rotting my connections. There can be no relief until words can once more breathe as before and again make their presence felt, until sounds and ink marks recover something of their meaning. It's getting late. I don't want to think about her. Somewhere, right now, her hands are moving, her facial muscles, her little feet. Somewhere real, I mean, out there, as well as in these ailing heartbeats where they're never absent. As for the rest, a lobotomy as the supreme goal, the television, the cell phone switched off, and the doors locked in a rage, slammed shut, the bolt slid all the way in. Locking the door from the inside like never before in my life. If anything's ailing me, it's my brain. I beg the memories to leave me be, in vain I call on the howls from the basement to fall silent once and for all. To no avail. I imagine that it might be possible to caress a living brain, to massage it gently, aside, I mean, from the way music or whispers sometimes do, metaphorically speaking, and I picture a hand with painted nails lightly touching my brain as I sit here, eyes closed, motionless, like when a stranger shaves you with a straight razor. The hand anoints me with oils, aromas, and ointments, daubing everything with fresh pomades, running its fingertips over my exhausted, wounded brain, very slowly, its folds, its darkest nooks and crannies, one by one, the blood vessels, taking care so as not to burst them and leave everything more blood-soaked than it already is.

Days, too, of pills to summon sleep if nothing else will work when the time comes to assuage that stubborn sorrow that festers within. No oriental poetry, or vanilla-scented candles, or listening to the music from before this whole disaster was unleashed, when everything was as it should be and the anxiety amounted to nothing more than what was basically feigned vulnerability, a way of being in the world, chosen freely, that had to do with the aesthetics of pessimism, the echoes of a half-understood Schopenhauer resounding in the background, like a cello hidden in the shadows, and that gorgeous, dark universe, brimful of poisons and solitary passersby, Brassaï's whores, the solitary drinkers of Picasso or Degas, fiery liquor, rain falling in back alleys, a blues sending a sudden shiver down the spine on the iciest of nights. Until, little by little, I dozed off, while I caressed my arms and shoulders, whispering Cavafy's "Body, Remember" to myself, that ravishing prayer of world-weary lovers, of those who sleep alone, now too late, come a certain age, but always accompanied by the memory of a bygone age crammed full of battles of love on long-gone nights, on hundreds of fitted sheets of all sizes and colors that bore in the form of a silhouette the traces of our most devoted sweat, and in the graffiti-filled restrooms of seedy dives and in cars parked beneath the trees, and in haylofts broken into with a kick to the door, atop piles of hay, and once or twice under silvery canopies, the ice bucket within reach and candles lit until dawn. Puzzling remnants of a memory that sometimes returns, albeit unbidden, powerful and stubborn, in the darkness of poorly ventilated bedrooms that now smell only of a very different sort of sweat and of cough syrups and viruses and an evening gown stored inside a trunk.

Either way, the dejection into which that breakup had plunged me was due not so much to my perception of the present, which, truth be told, concerned me little at that point, but rather to the image it offered up of my own past, of every faltering step up to that point, in one fell swoop stripping them bare of any hope of meaning. There is a fairly universal, recurring childhood nightmare in which the child calls out to those dearest to him, his mother, his father, who nevertheless act as if they hadn't seen him, talking to one another, going about their business, walking straight past him. This was quite similar, the feeling of shouting "it's me, don't you recognize me? I'm him, the same as ever, can't you see me?" but having the eyes you're seeking pierce straight through you without a second glance, like an unseeing sword, and your words sound just like those of a madman who dreamt the whole thing up, who made up a life no one can recall, one that rings false to the whole world, although your wrinkles are proof that, much to your regret, time has indeed passed. The dreadful part was not the sudden discovery that what I had for so long held to be the most important piece in the jigsaw of my life story had been plucked from my grasp, just like that, overnight, with such wounding ease, but rather the dawning realization that when something or someone truly ruins your life, it does so for good; we tend to think of our lost years in terms of the time left behind, but what is truly awful are the lost years that lie ahead. All that is to come will arrive more pallid and watered down, if not stillborn. I could now clearly see the enormous fragility of everything that had until recently appeared indestructible to my eyes. It was not being alone that pained me but rather the certainty that, one way or another, I now always would be, for I would be unable to see any woman who might at some point wish to approach me, no matter how naked, no matter how transparent her gaze, as anything other than the indifferent, absent-minded stranger she would sooner or later no doubt become, a stranger affecting to pretend that nothing really matters, that I never meant a thing, walking on different sidewalks in this city of mine, going in and out, at different times, of shops and bars I frequent, walking straight past my front door without even noticing, someone for whom I will one day have died without having died, much as I am now dead, without a funeral, without a homeland, barely a thing to call my own, in an asymmetrical parting of ways in which the burden of mourning lies only with the one who leaves—all of the tears are inside the casket, none are shed outside the coffin, out there springtime growls like a panther in heat and the time that remains calls to mind a party just about to begin.

And it's hard to die sometimes, especially when beyond that dark frontier, on the other side of the barbed wire laid out in the shadows, in place of respite what lies in wait are once again the days and the weariness, the work, the air aching inside the chest. To leave and to remain, that's the unbearable thing, to remain but to have left. As Celan put it in "Memory of France": "We were dead and we could breathe." Dead behind the gaze, which has not yet dimmed, behind eyes that continue to survey the stage, even when it now appears as barren as a snow-bound plain, a labyrinth in the form of an esplanade, or a ghost town with its dried-up water pipes, its abandoned train stations, the clumps of grass growing between the tracks, temples filled with cobwebs as if in a post-nuclear age, air of unwanted extra time, a handful of pages added slapdash to a worn-out tale. Dead, we sometimes run into others, perhaps also unsteady on their feet, groping their way in the dark, in a daze, as they roam their own invisible passageways in the midst of the fog, but we don't even see them, we can't see them, for this strange death, like the old Aristotelian god, is thought thinking itself, nothing but a feverish, obsessive loop.

Even so, there is something comforting in the idea of giving in to death, of relaxing one's muscles at last after long days of titanic struggle and simply giving up the fight. Taking to bed to die is a splendid thing. Before you know it, the mind has sketched in the details of a hotel room, a receiver resting precariously atop a telephone on the bedside table, the scent of Chanel N°5 on naked flesh. A crueler than cruel world on the other side of the window pane, a beautiful wound, a fragility that at long last gives in and succumbs to whatever may come, a gentle being that can take it no longer. In the adjacent bathroom, on the other side of a half-open door with white frames and golden doorknobs, stands a foam-filled tub, some of the candles on its rim still burning. When that mound of foam has finally gone completely cold, death will have arrived. In the meantime, only the pillow smelling of glycerin soap or the softener sold wholesale to the hotel chain. The watch still on the strap, the thin gold chain still slung around the neck, the breathing getting steadily deeper, dreams already flying over childhood streets, the escape attempts back then, a dilapidated grammar school in the neighborhood of Tetuán, the margarine and chorizo sandwiches made with yesterday's bread, the waste ground where on Saturday mornings I would transform into striker José Eulogio Gárate, the thirst, the fruit trees in summer, the waterholes, the brambles, the scent of fig trees, their sap as thick as an ogre's semen, the thorns of blackberry and rose bushes, knees stained with the red of Mercurochrome, the stones hurled in my direction, the homesick nights on Boy Scout camping trips (my city without me, far off, lit up in the middle of a plain, beyond those barren slopes, the interminable ranks of thickets and black hills under the moonlight), the sailor knots, the days that take their time, the bitter almonds. And also all that came in its wake: the insults, the vertigo and the nausea, the night as the realm of barking and eyes opened wide in the dark, behind every rock, hanging from the branches, watching from everywhere; the old, inevitable longing for every escape down endless highways or without moving from the spot, taking flight in the mind, throttling foes, smashing chains and locks in a rage, escaping from the fever, the aching bones, the shame; and the yearning, too, horribly insane, for all manner of poisons, hideouts, and underworlds, Bataille there, his verses borrowed one more time, one last time, *tu es l'horreur de la nuit, je t'aime comme on râle,* I love you as one might breathe one's last. You are the immensity of the fear. To see reflected in the monster's fangs the mouth you loved in times gone by, and in its claws the fingers of water that once sliced open your heart like a sweet blade. And *Verrà la morte e avrà i tuoi occhi.* And the vague sensation, in the watered-down images of delirium, that that which is dreadful is losing its bite while beauty sprouts claws and it is all much of a muchness and nothing truly matters any more.

That idea of slipping between the sheets, fresh from showering with the most expensive body wash, one last time, is not without its charm. One can snuggle up to it, that idea, hugging it as a child might embrace his rag doll in bed or an insomniac might clamp a sleeping pill beneath his tongue, with that same desperation and tenderness, and sensing the gentleness with which, from within, slowly, death washes over you. To erase, much like Borges's suicide, every thing and the sum of all things: "Not a single star will be left in the night. The night will not be left." To slowly forget it all, the blows, the slights, the most recent and the oldest scars, pink, hypertrophied. To sense the scent of Ruben Dario's funeral wreaths drawing ever closer, the cold wax, the black velvet, and also Juan Ramón Jimenez's birds, those that are going to stay, singing, beyond the window. And in the last instant to forgive God, to love the ruins for want of anything else, the waste left behind, the shards, the future like a treasure map burning in the bath, and to contemplate, with the indulgence that only weariness can give, with a gaze as tender as possible, the consummation of so much disaster. Yet it is not unheard of in such circumstances to weigh up the possibility of replacing that sterile agony with something that packs a greater punch. Something weighty, something grand, sublime if possible. It's only human and is a common occurrence; it's not unusual for the trick question to emerge unbidden: If the hardest part has already been established—the refusal to carry on with life as we knew it—if we have already said farewell to it all and that goodbye was heartfelt, then why not make the most of that extremely rare, formidable freedom, that impossible detachment that lies out of reach by any other means, to do that which, out of fear, was left undone? The worst failure, death itself, is already a given. In fact, it was half an hour away just moments ago, with all the bottles of pills laid out on the bedside table, as if on display. In such thoughts lie the true and invincible strength of the kamikaze, the courage of the hero who lays down his life, and the fearless energy of he who understands that the new dawn now means nothing to him, that its dirty light is no longer any concern of his, that time now is a vast foreign land, and who takes up residence in borrowed time that leaves him well placed, should he so wish, to bellow with laughter at it all, even that which he most feared, to be without being, to open the floodgates and drain himself of caution and shame in a hemorrhage that takes with it plans and resentments, long-held dreams, dread and pride. Many doors open from here on in, a whole world of possibilities that nevertheless have in common the power of that bitter, untamed freedom, the triumphant detachment of a spirit newly freed from instinct who has just lifted the veil that concealed a heady world. There are less pitiful ways to toy with self-destruction that lying on a bed, valium coming out of your ears: *Leaving Las Vegas*-style, for example, spending every last dime on the most expensive drinks, surrounded by whores and neon lights; or jotting down in a notebook, like in *My Life Without Me*, a list of the things that were left undone, little whims and flights of fancy, such as watching the dawn break in such and such a place or contemplating the sunset on the opposite side of the world, breakfasting on champagne and oysters, say, diving in the Caribbean, or running barefoot through the snow under a full moon, whatever. All of which is to suppose that there is any point in doing that which cannot be repeated or remembered, much less told. Pure performance for no one's eyes, like a poem written on a lost rock in a language mankind has long forgotten.

And then there is the option of being someone else, or at least pretending to be, of emigrating with the shirt on your back to anywhere on the far side of the ocean, to Mexico City, say, where fear roams the streets in green, panic-stricken taxis, at any time and heading who knows where, and everything is wild and speaks the truth. To touch down there one day, to put myself up again in the *Hotel Milán*, paying for a couple of nights at most to gather strength before setting out to beg on the streets until my heart bursts, collecting cardboard boxes, descending into the depths of hell, filling sheets of paper much like Jean Genet and good old Jean-Paul Clêbert, who, in his tiny, cramped handwriting, on any wrapper at all, even on crumpled cigarettes packs, scribbled down the exploits of the drifter's life, its wretched poetry, all that naïf drivel about life beneath a star-studded canopy, but also the rush of refusing to contemplate anything other than life as it is lived in the moment, the heart beating now, the dinner and the roll in the hay that very night, the just stolen wine washing down the throat like a blessing, the company at once dangerous and endearing of those who barely question themselves underneath the world's sewers. Changing continents is about as close as I can imagine coming to her never having been born.

I could perhaps make my way to Zipaquirá, just as I've sometimes thought about doing. In that Colombian city, on my return from Vilha de Leiva, in the taxi taking us back to Bogota one Sunday evening, I saw myself. And with such clarity that I had no time to react or ask our driver to pull over a moment to the curb. In the slums of Zipaquirá, in a sort of makeshift roadside bar made from materials like tarpaulin, plywood, and tin, where liquor and bottles of beer were served on the edge of the highway, I spotted myself, utterly weather beaten, unsteady on my feet, clutching a drink in one hand. It was me. And for a moment I saw myself twice over—from my car seat, I saw that outcast with unkempt hair, drinking what might have been mescal by the side of the road, and, from that very same curb and with equal astonishment, I saw my reflection seated inside a taxi bound for the capital, its trunk laden with the bags of *longaniza* we had just bought in Zutamarchán. I've seen myself on other occasions, albeit more hazily and in static images—a snapshot of a group of prisoners in the barracks of Auschwitz taken by the allied soldiers, the camp newly liberated, among the figures in a painting by Ramón Casas—in which, with the passing of time, the likeness has slowly faded. I have never, however, stopped toying with the idea of going back to look for myself in that lost city in the region of Cundinamarca. No one will ever fully convince me that the drunkard in Zipaquirá, who was struck, just as I was, half-dead with astonishment on seeing me drive past, was not me.

But for the most part, such thoughts amount to little more than an excuse, almost always compelling, to tumble from your bed and crawl over to the phone, praying that it's not too late to have your stomach pumped. The ambulances, the lights, the world hurtling back into view, tearing the black cobwebs to shreds. A niggling doubt will suffice, though we know full well that such globe-trotting plans to embark on part two of our lives, now free from meaning and our former concerns, are little more than a long line of unspent bullets, booby traps, phantasmagorias, pipe dreams that are the product of a mind that refuses to resign itself to mingling with the earth just yet. Out of self-interest and an instinct for survival, the unconscious tends to keep its lips sealed as tight as a whore's even when it's as clear as day how such adventures will end, the vengeance-seeking self-sacrifice that strikes us as laughable, if not worse, the following morning, the list in a notebook that will never even be bought, the flights never taken, the planes that take to the air without us on board, just as thousands do every day at every latitude and in every possible direction, a white trail in their wake, slicing across the sky at all hours of the day and bearing our empty seat, touching down beneath rain showers that will never drench us on the outskirts of cities filled with alleyways down which we will never lose our way and women with whom we will never exchange so much as a glance, let alone fluids or promises.

Greatness, true luxury, lies in that somewhat aristocratic disdain, not in the worst sense of the word, of always doing things by halves—the tumbler of brandy left partly undrunk on the terrace of a bar, the coins not fully gathered up from the dish on which the waiter has brought the change from your order, the last bits of sauce not mopped up, whole evenings of drowsiness and complacency, wasted without guilt for there is more than enough life to go around, because there's plenty of time yet. This is the attitude that stands in contrast to that of the miserable wretch driven by the most visceral and tight-fisted need to see poetry in the idea of draining every last drop of what life has to offer. And so he throws nothing away, and saves for a rainy day, stingily hoarding the leftovers to be polished off later, much as a dog that has had its fill might bury bones next to a tree so as not to let a single ounce of food go to waste, and he dunks every last *churro* in his order of hot chocolate, no matter that he's full to bursting, whether or not he has any room left in his belly. It's a thousand times better to always leave a little something on the plate, to thumb your nose elegantly at part of the banquet, to dine, say, with a ravishing lady and gracefully allow her to escape with her life. And, in that same haughty vein, to abandon life at the midway point, to up and leave, just like that, as one might leave untouched what remains of an ice-cream cone now melted or a saucer bearing loose change.

43

Yet the mind is wont to erase such ideas at a stroke, much as it silences other questions that do perhaps matter when talk turns to escape: If you shatter all the crockery against the wall, how will you then blow off steam in future? If you sever all ties, what bonds will you then shrug off? If you abandon all point of reference, from where or from what can you now retreat? And the clincher, the central refrain of a woebegone song of destitution and abandonment that refuses to fade out altogether in your head: To what end your footsteps through the world, the new cities, the seas you cross, the paths you take, the horizons, the storms through which you pass and which pass through you, the fruits you grasp, your glory or your downfall, your wretched self lost in the desert of what lies ahead, if the eyes that once looked on your life are now closed?

4

(man overboard)

Christmas is the hardest time of year to get some time to yourself. There are people who call you at all hours to make sure you're OK and aren't festering in gloom during the holidays. They will not leave you be. They sign you up for dinners, they insist on taking you out on the town. I felt the need for a quick trip, to get a little distance from it all, and so it was that my 2010 began in Paris, a plastic cup in my hand and party music boring into my brain under an Eiffel Tower lit up in dazzling, electric blue. Thousands of people taking snapshots of the metallic chill and the effect of the laser beams on the steel and the sky, while dozens of hooded, tattooed youths lined up against every wall in a large, cordoned-off radius to be patted down by the police, hands behind their heads, feet spread as far apart as possible. In the neighboring streets, cars burned amid the sound of sirens and puddles of champagne.

It was fiercely cold the following day. Beneath the snowflakes that fell as if in slow motion, I walked the two or three blocks that separated my hotel from Montparnasse

Cemetery, then whiled away a couple of hours between its walls, pausing before the same graves that had drawn me to them the first time I had set foot there several years before—the graves of Duras, Cortázar, Vallejo, Baudelaire—this time adding to my brief itinerary a couple of tombstones to which I had before paid little heed, pausing also before the grave of Serge Gainsbourg, covered with flowers, rain-sodden cigarettes, handwritten notes, and miniature bottles of liquor, and that of Jean Seberg, the lone huntress, who finally secured her spot beneath the funereal earth at the eighth request. Squatting on my haunches in front of each one, running my fingertips over the damp slabs as if the marble might offer up something akin to an answer, musing vaguely on the way of things and again wondering why it is that even my deepest desires, even when they go hand in hand with urgency, fury, or maelstrom, always materialize with a question mark. Sensing the perfume of the black roses, of the giant petals I cannot recognize, all of the sorrow laid out there, in the true heart of the world, around the cypresses, beneath the snow, beneath the stone, beneath all of the footsteps, beneath everything.

Paris was nothing more than a boulevard of ashes, so whispered Moustaki to my adolescent self from a red plastic battery-powered cassette player as I lay on my bed, at a time when the world's cities first began to take shape in my mind, with their bridges, their secret places, and their towers, based on three or four photos I had stumbled upon and music aplenty. And that, a boulevard of ashes, was precisely what the streets were to me until I reached the Mirabeau Bridge. I had no way of knowing which side Paul Celan had leapt from on the night of the 19th to the 20th of April, 1970, and so I picked one at random and stood there a good long while, gazing at the water. I have never set much store by the time-honored metaphor that holds that life is a river that carries us along. Rather it strikes me that if time is pushing us onward, it does so while at the same time passing through us, wearing us down, transforming us from head to toe. It is not a question of the current simply carrying us, just as we are, from one spot to another, closer to the sea or to death with each passing minute. If there is no escaping the hours and days, tomorrow or the past, this is because yesterday has warped us, that's all there is to it; it has taken us from A to B, leaving within us traces of calamity and weariness. I'd be lying if I said that my footsteps had led me to that bridge purely by chance. Peering over those railings had been the main reason for my trip to Paris. In order to arrive at or manufacture that moment, I had crossed the Pyrenees two days previously, catching a high-speed train in Pau with the sole intention of standing there a good long while, watching the water enter the arch of the bridge only to disappear behind my back, bound for the ocean. It's strange how we sometimes choose the places in which to find answers or a simple tonic to ease the sorrow that possesses us, or to which vanquished gods we beg for light, the baffling way in which we scour the world for altars to kneel before and sacred moments, dubious symbols, gazes that take naked snapshots of us from up on high in a broken sky. As I contemplated the current from that spot, imagining the thunderous sound made by a body dropping like a stone from the railings at an hour when the whole world is asleep, I was in fact seeking to find out whether or not, when push came to shove, I wished to carry on living. Or, more to the point, whether or not I would carry on living. This was what had brought me there, although I believe that I could never, at that point or ever, have put a finger on quite why.

Those days, my inner devastation was complete, and I was bogged down in a state of uselessness that was dragging on longer than was desirable. My finances had run aground, everyday work had become a hellish affair, and my former excesses and the anxiety of that time, with its poor sleep and even worse diet, with all of its despair and pharmacopoeia, had started—prone to dying as I've always been—to take its toll on my body. I spent my time in the hotel reading. I had taken plenty of books but couldn't settle on a single one, flitting from one to another, on edge, as one might when hunting for an urgent piece of information. I underlined the following passage in my copy of Sándor Márai's *Diaries*: "Did I love her? I don't know. Can one love one's legs, one's thoughts? Quite simply, everything is meaningless without legs or thoughts. Without her, everything is meaningless—I do not know if I loved her. It was something else. I don't love my kidneys or my pancreas, either. They simply form part of me, just as she formed part of me." I thought about calling Jacobo to ask him a question or two about the urban backdrop to Celan's last days, but I couldn't bring myself to do so, for he would no doubt have picked up on the alarm signals in my tone of voice, and I figured him capable of putting together a rescue sortie in a matter of hours to come to my aid if he pictured me wandering aimlessly through those streets, alone, my gaze obliterated, heading from bar to bar, in such dangerous proximity to the bridges.

There are dreams that simply tear you asunder, a thousand times worse than any insomnia, no matter how sweat drenched or heart stopping, no matter how fiercely the temples throb. As a reader or observer of life, I have always been a sucker for the lure I spoke of earlier of situations in which someone has no choice but to start from scratch: tales of prisoners released back into the outside world with little but the shirts on their backs; exiles who return to their former neighborhoods after years of absence in search of any old job with which to get by and a temporary room in which to hang their hat; foreign widowers who appear out of nowhere; people who, overnight, for whatever reason, change their habits and their passport. I had always seen a whirlwind of light there, the irresistible rush of wiping the slate clean, of turning what had until then been a remote possibility into something that lives and breathes, of calmly pulling up a chair to ponder, without haste of any kind, in any old bar in the recently unveiled world, who one will be from that moment on, the battles to be waged once more, and even, by extension, the fears that will from now on quicken the pulse in the midst of a ravaged landscape that is, at one and the same time, the cradle of all that is to come. Now that it was I, however, who found myself in such a fix, I couldn't shake the feeling that I had fallen by the wayside, sick and sapped of strength for any further adventures for the time being. All the same, the old urge to take flight was triggered, the same one that had led me to drive hour after hour down Spain's highways every summer, aimless and heading nowhere in particular, listening to country records, stopping to rest at gas stations, and jotting down vague musings in a small notepad. Only this time it was triggered in a much more scattershot, painful way, for this now had nothing to do with that old affectation of scribbling on maps or looking for hotels as desolate and cinematographic as possible in which to spend the night, with a broken down ice machine, tattered blinds, and desolation in the form of damp patches on the wallpaper if possible. All that had before amounted to little more than a gentle gloom had now become spiderwebs and trembling. Those thousand-mile getaways bore about as much resemblance to this flight that had now begun as a child pretending to be killed by a shot to the chest does to one dying for real on the sidewalk, the whites of his eyes showing.

Yet there is a dark pleasure to be had in setting fire to ships and watching as any hope of return goes up in flames on the water, a mile from the shore. Once the thought has crossed your mind, it's hard to resist the temptation to make a clean break, the longing to give in to the black vortex that seeks to swallow you whole from inside an abyss, like a giant claw grabbing you by the ankles and dragging you in; it's tough to give up on the idea of cutting the ropes and turning off the lights, unplugging everything so that all that remains is to toss portraits, bouquets, and ashes overboard. You know you shouldn't yet are powerless to do otherwise. Just like when, as a child, you strike a younger brother just because you feel like it, or dump the girl of your dreams for no reason she or anyone else can grasp, leaving her, just like that, weeping on a park bench.

A few days after having officially left, I had to return to my former apartment to fetch a few of my belongings when I spotted a pair of my shoes—dirty, somewhat the worse for wear, in need of a lick of polish—lying forlornly on the bedroom floor. For some obscure reason, a pair of shoes always makes my thoughts turn to death. At some point in my childhood, perhaps not as hazy in my nightmares as I might like to think in my waking hours, I must have been taken aback on entering the room of a dead relative, one of those distant family members who would pass away in provinces as lost as they themselves were, forcing me to travel all night long and miss a day of school among the cypresses, the black-clad women brewing endless pots of coffee, and all manner of friends and in-laws trying on the deceased man's overcoats for size, almost out of eyeshot. And I'd swear that after the funeral, I spotted a pair of black shoes on the floor and understood death on sensing, for the very first time, the absence of any legs rising up toward the bedroom ceiling, forming a human being along the way, with his gestures and his white shirt; the void left behind by the dead man was right there, in the air above the shoes. And, stricken with horror, I also sensed the prospect of widowed foot-steps roaming the hallways in the nights to come. The shoes lay a few short yards from the bed that, though it might now smell only of fever, and though pictures of the Virgin Mary had been pinned to the headboard, had no doubt in the not too distant past been privy to laughter and desire—the door locked from the inside entirely by design and the children horsing around on the other side of it, hovering dangerously close, the sweet fear of being caught in the act, the mischief of urgent lovemaking. I knew, as soon as I clapped eyes on those discarded shoes of mine, that I was a dead man in that house. In other words, it was as if between those four walls there languished a ghost whose facelessness was precisely my facelessness. The sight of that footwear tipped the balance more than the sight of empty closets with bare coat hangers, barren drawers, or bookshelves covered in nothing but dust. In Auschwitz, so Jacobo had taught me, shoes were piled up at the entrance and can still be seen in the camp quarters that now house a museum. A huge heap of loafers, boots of all types and sizes, children's sandals. Contemplating that colossal pile, you think of the barbarity, of numbers and facts and the horror of history, of the pajama-clad skeletons filing past in black and white that we've seen in so many documentaries, all those trains screeching to a halt at the gates to hell; but if you pause awhile to observe one single item of footwear, one shoe in particular or a pair tethered together by a knot, then you see the dead child. You see a boy struggling to tie the laces in order to keep the boot from falling off with every step he takes or from swallowing up his socks. You picture him seated on the ground, tugging firmly on the tongue of his shoe, you see his snot, you hear his breathing, the sound of his lungs compressing the frozen air of a Polish winter. Just as I saw myself in that apartment. When I closed the door behind me, the shoes stayed where they were, empty forevermore, foolish, bereft, filled with air getting staler with each passing minute. My life, from that moment onward, was something else, something hard to pin down, the exploits of a being who moved outside of myself, and barefoot. At that moment, my mood was abject. The streets, the world, any room in which I might find myself, had become pure exposed terrain.

I've had that same sense of my own death on returning to cities or neighborhoods from my past, any of the places from which I'd vanished without a trace and which have carried on regardless, the everyday hustle and bustle, bars that change owners, stores that shut down, streets that are widened, neon signs where before there was nothing. It's no stretch to see yourself as a ghost among neighbors who no longer recognize you, the handful of storekeepers who remain behind their counters, affable and grown old as if by magic, the groups of kids who appear out of nowhere, making their way home from school amid a clamor of shouts and snacks wrapped in tinfoil and soccer balls and schoolbooks with homework for the following day, the clusters of women chatting on the sidewalk, and the pitiful cries of the lottery vendors. That pair of shoes lying on the floor brought home the fact that, for all intents and purposes, I had just died for many people. Without the grieving of others, without the slightest ritual, but with the exact same outcome of dark solitude and absence stretching out as far as the eye could see. My thoughts turned to the names of all those I would never again see, save some freak occurrence, all those individuals who, without my ever having been truly close to them, had nevertheless formed the human backdrop against which my days unfolded. Without the spotlight of their gaze on me, everything took on a nightmarish air. What becomes of a life when no one is watching anymore, aside from a nonentity who comes and goes, eats dinner or doesn't, squirms or laughs? If, when all is said and done, every life is a story, then every story needs a reader. Otherwise, the world around us runs the risk of fading to nothing, leaving behind nothing more than disjointed perceptions, moments like islands, brief snatches. True destitution arises when we exit the stage and the eyes that followed our movements vanish or explode or simply take to the air like tiny balloons fleeing to the skies of other worlds. Certain parallels can be drawn between the newly abandoned and that classmate orphaned in primary school with whom we all wished to share part of our sandwiches during recess, trying to make sure he was not left all alone with his thoughts in the corner: the un-ironed shirt, the gaze perpetually lost in the distance, and that almost imperceptible dampness pooled in the corners of the eyes. But at least he had a star on which to gaze at night from his bedroom, or so he said, and that same star watched over his footsteps and sometimes even quizzed him on the lesson of the following day. For the one who's been jilted, instead, the blackness of the sky is filled only with closed eyelids. A vast drawn curtain. When the mannequin is moved from the shop window to the storeroom in the far end of the basement, it matters little what clothes it's wearing, whether or not it's broken, whether or not it still trembles.

From Paris, at a distance of so many miles, I was seeking to get a clear view, from another vantage point, of the recent events in my life and the state of mind in which I found myself, while trying, as far as possible, to put things back in some sort of order. I had just moved into a tenth-floor apartment from which I could see the towers on the Cathedral of Our Lady of Pilar and one or two other high-rises that gave the city skyline a Mudejar air. A welcoming spot, with plenty of wood, just as I've always liked, plaster bas-reliefs even in the bathroom, and festooned with Japanese ornaments, prints, and plates with painted birds hanging on the walls. The street was on a slope, and the city buses hurtled by, heading downhill to the center of town or skidding alarmingly to a halt in front of the bus shelter that stood on the opposite sidewalk. Sometimes, at night, the noise got mixed up in my slumbers with the sound of a cliff top suddenly crumbling. The bedding and the table linen were the most characterful items in that apartment, everything as if from a bygone age, as if stolen from an imaginary museum dedicated to my childhood. A female friend who dropped by from time to time back then to spice up my siestas a little bought me a new set of bedsheets—"I sleep in this bed of yours and I feel like my own mother or something. I can't fuck like this." Though I began using the sheets she had brought, in deference to her, the others were more to my liking. I explained to her that even in Barcelona, most apartments are like this on the inside, I'd seen them. Later, you'd spot their occupants out and about, sporting their designer gear, wearing those gray shirts or riding their bikes, a Nike backpack or a leather bag slung over their shoulders. Which is all well and good, but their apartments are just like this on the inside. Most are, anyway. Flick any switch, and desolation lights up on the ceiling. On the six-bulb chandeliers, two or three bulbs at most work, and they give off a light so yellowish and washed out it's almost enough to make you wish you were dead, if only so as not to belong, as though you were just one more item among all the others, to the collection of things surrounding you, all taking up a certain volume of air, just like you—everything: crochet circles, porcelain objects, faded towels folded in two in the top drawer of a closet that doesn't quite close right.

The children would sometimes come by on Fridays. They'd arrive bearing a ton of luggage to spend the weekend. The refrigerator empty. Me barely able to get a word out. They took in their surroundings and exchanged glances before finally turning to face me. I guess the question that hung in the air was something like *now what do we do?* Not in terms of that particular moment, but rather from now on, *what are we going to do, how are we going to manage now that everything we once were has come apart at the seams?* With all the suitcases lying around, the travel bags stuffed with changes of clothes, pajamas, and small toys, the backpacks with homework for school, the overcoats lying in a heap, we looked like the surviving members of a family in a refugee camp. It was as if their mother had been killed in an air raid and the three of us, before fleeing, had spotted her dead body peeking out from among the ruins, her white lips stuck to the earth, her hair matted with lime scale, a hazy cloud of flies and dust. I asked myself what right I had to make them breathe the air of that tormented world of mine, the silence, the books strewn on the floor, the grime in the corners, whether I had anything other than sorrow to offer them. And I wondered if a dead father might not be preferable to a downtrodden father falling to pieces before your eyes while you're powerless to do anything, unable to understand a thing. We would go out for a stroll every now and then, swaddled in scarves and without quite knowing where we were heading. The two of them always trailing behind, following mother duck, bursting with questions but never daring to articulate a single one. Sometimes I would take the little one's hand and squeeze it tight. Rather than affection or the sense of security he no doubt needed, I feel that this gesture served only to convey the unwanted lesson that there is no such thing, when all is said and done, as love without weeping, time without emptiness, or flesh without tearing, and that the defeated man he now saw before him is how things always turn out when you set your heart with sufficient fervor on something, whatever it may be. In his eyes, the figure of a protective father had no doubt vanished for good, his place taken by another creature, familiar and unknown in equal measure, as lost as he was and cornered by a sorrow that mirrored his own. The scene reminded me of a fairly well-known photograph by Manuel Ferrol that has for some reason been etched in my memory ever since I first saw it and somehow sums up the mood of those first weekends in the company of my children, one called *Émigrés' Farewell*, taken in La Coruña in '56. It's not clear whether father and son are about to go their separate ways any minute or are saying goodbye to a third person just out of shot. A rough hand attempts to embrace the child with tenderness, although it does so with great awkwardness. The two of them are crying and looking straight ahead, perhaps at the gangway of a ship. Though in our case there were no ships, or sea, or anything in sight, everything that surrounded us was shot through with that air of a dockside farewell and the certainty that someone or something was stealing, from under our very noses, a huge shipment of things we would never see again. Perhaps my son, even as I embraced him, saw his father leaving.

How long does it take for a man to die, lying on the bed without another thought in his head, staring at the ceiling, determined not to budge an inch, not to eat, to let buzzers and phones go unanswered? How long before the tears on his face dry up? At what precise moment do the relevant ducts run dry and cease flowing? There is a type of madness akin to a black nausea that tends to spread upward to the brain. Sometimes this happens at such speed that it takes on the unmistakable air of a fit of insanity. This is what happens to the occasional somewhat half-heartedly suicidal individual, as well as certain murderers of the sort that repent straight away, no sooner has the deed been done, who ask themselves what they've done and call the police themselves, covering the corpse laid out on the floor with kisses, drenching it with snot and words. In my case, the froth of that retching takes somewhat longer to rise. It starts in the gut and advances in slow waves like a thick foam before taking up residence among the folds of my brain, flooding that uncharted viscosity with images of skulls, and memories, and loathing, inserting the word *death* into every thought, with a shoe horn if need be, not as a crystal-clear concept but rather as the hazy outline of a rusty scythe or a cross driven into the earth in the midst of the trembling. And it's hard then to pull yourself together, for the vantage point from which you survey the world retreats from the present moment and takes up position somewhere so dark that time becomes a murderous, nimble entity and death, or signs that relentlessly bring it to mind, is everywhere you look; for example, try as I might, I couldn't stop myself from seeing some of my female friends who often dropped by the apartment in those days not as they were there and then but rather how I imagined they might be on reaching old age, and myself as a more or less banal episode from their past. Beneath their current flesh, I could already see an old woman beginning to emerge, sighing wearily while waiting in line at some market or other, for whom someone, perhaps I myself, had laid out their medicines on the bedside table. The beginnings of the odd wrinkle here and there foreshadowed a face that was not yet a reality but that I was powerless to ward off, also affecting their breath, the way they carried themselves, and the way they fell silent. In the case of Julia, it didn't stop there; I found it impossible to be by her side without picturing her naked skull and the tomb that would sooner or later house all those bones, the pubis that ground itself against me in a frenzy, the spread-eagled femurs, the worn-out shinbones that circled my waist, the jawbone that set upon my mouth in the darkness. I feel that the idea of death is like a giant crow, or any other carrion bird with huge wings like oily capes that's able to smell sorrow from a long way off, as if it were incense dissolved in the air, and draws near whenever someone looks weak, in order to lurk close by and, depending on the conviction with which the wounded man blindly flails, to peck timidly or tear into flesh for which no one yearns.

The lifeless body of Paul Celan was fished out from a quiet spot on the Seine six miles downstream. I felt I was already halfway down a similar route. All that remained was to wait and see which riverside branch might snag my legs. A shoe would no doubt detach itself to continue its journey oceanward, like a small grave boat. I thought of someone gathering up the body and of the possibility that a breath of air might bring me back to life. But I did not, in the end, jump from any bridge. Not that time.

I took to my bed early that night in my room at the Hôtel du Nord, as the sleet continued to fall in the interior courtyard onto which my window looked, and the TV news kept replaying the same images of cars set ablaze the night before, seats burnt to a cinder, puddles of gasoline, warped scrap metal. I remember closing my eyes, then running my fingers though my own hair, imagining that my hand belonged to someone else, anyone, someone who knows that my heart is filled with bitter wells into which they do not entirely want to peer, nor look the other way, either, and who tells me, as sleep slowly comes, that there are cities in the world in which day has already broken, where people are beginning to head outdoors, fresh from the shower, to buy some bread and the morning papers and grab a freshly roasted coffee and buttered toast with marmalade on the terraces of the corner bars, and who speaks to me of the sun breaking through the most wayward of clouds and the treetops, reassuring me, in barely more than a murmur, that little by little, without my realizing, I will gather together the pieces and reassemble, with what little remains, something resembling a human being. You'll see. I'll see. And I doze off a few blocks from a vast river, beneath a cracked sky, in the room of a two-bit hotel where no one who knows me is aware I'm staying, hidden by the shadows of a boulevard not too far from the ranks of burnt-out cars, not so many yards from my lost footsteps. Resting means that no one can see me.

5

(other people's fear)

Around about the date of my return from that trip came
the period when Jacobo began to feel afraid at night. Very
afraid, I mean, like a sort of extra helping on top of what he
had felt, as a matter of course, his entire life. He could not
bring himself to be alone. Sometimes he feared he would
once again dream of the ghosts of Gestapo officers, hustling
him from office to office before forcing him on board a
train that crossed snow-covered forests, but for the most part
he was afraid of more voracious, vaguer horrors. He would
call me as the afternoon neared its end and summon me to
his side. And so, without much of a fuss, I would toss my
pajamas, a transistor radio with headphones, a toiletry bag,
and a couple of books I had into a small backpack, and
before long, I'd turn up at his door. It was easy, I barely had
to lift a finger, and that's the sort of job that's always been
right up my alley. Truth be told, he didn't need looking after,
and his mental state was seemingly normal most of the time.
Indeed, on some nights you could say he was in particularly
good spirits, and it was not therefore a matter for urgency

or alarm. All that was asked of me was that I remain there, in his apartment, chatting idly about this, that, and the other, or each to his own, reading opposite one another, each man seated in his armchair, until we succumbed to sleep. It was by no means an unattractive proposition. Sometimes I'd sit there observing him, engrossed in his book and unaware that I was staring at him so openly—his close-cropped, graying hair, his air of a Reserve Marine, well into his sixties, equal parts affectionate and gruff, forever torn between those bottomless wells into which he would sink with increasing frequency and a certain *joie de vivre* that had to do above all with a love of art and fine wine, and a worship of women that might be described as not of this world; he even took pleasure in watching as they passed him by.

It's strange to stand guard over something you cannot see. My enemy there, on that house-bound mission, was supposedly the legion of ghosts that were filing through his head, something intangible, dark, slippery to the touch, creatures that roamed unchecked on a plane to which I had no direct access (nor did he, that was the problem) and that would all of a sudden make him suspect the presence, on the other side of the window, of snout-like things all set to explode in a snarling fury or gleaming blades that made him think of an artery sliced in half, although for the time being they were content simply to bide their time out there, behind the poplars gently rocking in the nighttime breeze or submerged in the pools of asphalt lit up in amber by the traffic lights flashing throughout the early hours of morning. A force without name or measure. I would have been of little use in the event of an attack. I felt in a way as if I formed part of the sentry of a medieval king, facing the possible arrival of an alien invasion that would descend from the skies at supersonic speed, unleashing laser beams left, right, and center from a flying saucer. Eyes watchful, bow string and muscles pulled taut, a fierce gesture, and nothing more. That's about it, little more than a token gesture of pointless loyalty, like the chanting of a crew as their ship goes inexorably under. I guess my presence was about as much use as a few drops of a placebo slipped slyly into his after-dinner glass of milk. But I realize that Jacobo did not call me so that I might air my opinion as to whether or not my dropping by was necessary or useful, but rather in order that I might heed his call, pure and simple; that's how it goes when anxiety begins to squirm in the guts or the trembling of a memory, which all of a sudden, deep down, takes on a monstrous form, setting off alarms for good reason or otherwise. "You have to come, my thoughts are aquiver again," he'd say, or, "I feel like I'm dying tonight." This was his way of putting a name to the fear that everything would fade to black with no one on hand to whom he might say goodbye, or of spending another night sitting on the edge of the mattress, clawing at his scalp, as had happened before. When push came to shove, matters rarely came to a head when I was around. At times the anxiety was a little shriller and brandished shadowy claws that were never actually put to use, while at others it was simply the gentle perception of a heart slowing down, a sadness like a faded afternoon, when tedium cloaks objects and memories, without distinction, in the same invisible fog in which desire cannot breathe.

This was not the first time someone had made such a request of me. I have had relatives who were afraid of dying alone, in the middle of the night, and I have turned up on their doorsteps carrying a similar backpack, with the same satisfaction at being of use without having to lift barely a finger, for in reality they are content just to hear your breathing, to sense the mild heat a human body gives off, the occasional household noise close by, anything will do—the coffee pot on the stove, the click of a lighter— and to know that you're on hand and will call the on-duty doctor, the ambulance, or whoever, should it come to that, or will at least squeeze their hand when the time comes to drift inevitably off to what they have occasionally glimpsed as a clinging darkness with no hope of return, when a sticky silence begins to pull them by the feet, dragging them with irresistible force from the other side of a sudden vertigo or the very sound of their galloping pulse. There ought to be some sort of protection for the mind, somehow, like a kind of sheepdog that, whenever one such venomous thought is about to venture into the swampy regions of the memory or project new forms of shadow or cobwebs, would herd it back together with the rest of the flock into some quiet enclosure bathed in light; it would tear the circle of obsession apart with its teeth, round up the stampeding ghosts, hunt them down through the labyrinths, sink its fangs into them until their veins of black juice burst once and for all or they were imprisoned in silence inside the pen.

In times gone by, many years ago now, I've also found myself on the other side. In other words, I was the one in dire need of a nearby presence so as not to succumb to panic. This was back in the toxic, hectic Madrid of the eighties, when my brain was a giant, raw wound inside my head. I remember my little mat laid out on the floor, at the foot of my friend Andrés's bed, when we shared an apartment in the Estrecho district, and how his steady breathing somehow helped me keep time with my own in an attempt to sleep. Truth is, there is little more that can be done. It is at such times that I have caught the clearest glimpse of the fundamental loneliness of a human being, any human being, and the impossibility of any real communication. There is no transplant of nerves or blood, no way of releasing that fear from its cage. Two people can even hold each other tight, clutching hands, yet one will never truly be able to penetrate the other's hell, or even remotely understand it. It's impossible. Beyond a rudimentary sense of empathy that all but ends with the certainty that the other is suffering—but this is just abstract—there is nothing that can be done to penetrate the other's thoughts, the other's fear, and to fight tooth and nail, as one might so often wish, against the ghosts and the storms that are gathering in there. There is a profound, painful truth to that vision of Goethe's whereby one's inner life is akin to a sort of fortified citadel that no one can ever truly breach or, for that matter, leave, though linguistic sleight of hand may conjure an illusion to the contrary. In the middle of the night, two friends embrace in their pajamas, they ruffle each other's hair, exchanging words of loyalty and encouragement, but only one is torn asunder, trembling inside, only one breaks out in an icy sweat.

Jacobo would sometimes try his hand at watercolor, usually vases of flowers, or fruit bowls, or candelabras, but also landscapes with outlandish skies, fearsome storms, or

Vettriano knockoffs, those women who emerge when night, sin, and silk entwine, who gaze off into the distance, a cigarette in their hand, fancying themselves the magnets of all desire. For me, one of life's great pleasures has always been to look on as someone paints or sketches at my side, acting as if I weren't there. It must, however, be someone who takes the matter seriously, not some half-hearted exercise that matters little one way or the other, for here the other person's passion is even more key to the performance than the outcome itself; and Jacobo, even though he ended up tearing almost every canvas to shreds, threw himself headlong into the task as if his life depended on it, head tilted to one side, tongue poking out like a schoolboy endeavoring to write out his first letters by hand, holding his sketch pad out in search of the right distance from which to gauge the play of texture, light, and line. If everything falls into place, I can be sent into a trance of sorts by the smell of pencils, ink, and oil paint and the sound of lead pencils and erasers on the paper. I can sometimes feel a shudder of delight up around the ears that takes me back to those dingy, old shoe repair shops, tiny and cramped, that were a regular feature in the neighborhoods of my childhood. Outside, the heavens have opened and the air in the street carries the scent of waves and sardines; there's a small glass-fronted den where a half-broken, staticky radio dripping with grease can be heard, along with the hammer blows of an old man struggling with a midsole, daubing it with glue, rummaging around for the exact size of nail through cluttered drawers in which finding anything seems an impossible task. Everything is awash with the penetrating aroma of those super-strength glues that, in turn, smell of a bygone industry, of Hernani and other northern factory towns in the seventies, and also, as if in passing, of a kid getting high, hunched over a plastic bag, seated on the edge of a sidewalk that lies on the other side of an Atlantic Ocean also perhaps battered into submission by the very same rain; and the perfume of leather and polish, of the yellowish light of the cozy hideout from which I hoped I would never be dragged away, praying to the heavens that the cobbler would take his time in seeing to the clients ahead of me, for some last-minute repair to be made on the spot, for some shoe that had slipped his mind and had to be returned without delay to the woman standing before me in line, or for some barefoot girl to enter, clutching a heel, pleading for assistance there and then, hopping on one leg, her tights soaked through, the nylon flecked with mud.

Our conversations often turned to literature; his entire living room was strewn with books, most arranged on dusty shelves, many other piled up in various heaps: those he had just read, those he planned to read, and those that flitted between the two piles for one reason or other. Many of them were bookmarked, with yellow notes signaling the paragraphs that in recent days Jacobo had thought he might read out loud to me, sometimes whole passages and sometimes, more often than not, brief snippets of something pithy or that had, for whatever reason, taken his fancy, underlined in pencil, by way of aphorisms that we might discuss as he whipped up something to eat—in his underwear, as usual, wearing his battered slippers. After painstaking rereadings of nineteenth and early twentieth century novels, as if to take a break from the thousands of pages of Proust, Baroja, and Thomas Mann's unbridled prose, he had recently decided to throw himself back into the poetry of Jabès and Celan, old acquaintances, and had even learned certain poems from *Poppy and Memory* and *No One's Rose* by heart, seeking out different translations that he later liked for the two of us to compare, though neither of us spoke a word of German. He tended to turn to poetry only when he was at his lowest ebb and could barely concentrate or even sit down to read without having to get up from his chair every other minute to pace up and down the hallway or fix himself something from the fridge or the drinks cabinet. He brought me up to speed on Celan's life story and his addictive verse. Indeed, thanks to him, I ended up drenched in the work of Celan, whom I began to picture always in the midst of a snowy landscape, a lump in his throat, the proprietor of an inhuman sadness and a feeling of guilt that never, not a single day in his life, allowed him to banish from his thoughts the image of his dead parents lying on the cold ground, in the Mikhailovka camp, on the banks of the Bug. The bullet hole in the back of his mother's head, the knowledge that he could have saved them, everything half-shrouded in a blanket of white. Jacobo managed to inject me with the poison of that delicacy. There are works that take you over like a virus. We carry them with us for a while, much like someone who has come down with an illness, then they slowly disappear, albeit leaving in their wake traces of what was once their way of gazing upon the world and things, and a handful of verses with all the flavor of what has seemingly been forgotten.

Aside from all the talk of books and reading, I hoped he might also tell me how things were on the female front, in part because that sort of conversation had always, in the past at least, ended up lifting his spirits, and also partly so that I myself might enjoy the women in his telling, beautiful as only they were, and who, in Jacobo's words, took dainty little steps, word by word, as if down the carpeted, hushed corridor of a ghostly hotel, toward glorious sin. He led me to believe that there was little to report in that regard, although certain aspects of his appearance—the frequency with which he shaved and the new wardrobe he had recently acquired—inclined me to think he was lying.

At the usual hour of my arrival at his apartment, the city outside was for Jacobo little more than an indeterminate threat that slowly waned as people at last holed themselves up in their lairs, a sort of fleeting false alarm or slumbering monster before which it would on no account do to lower one's guard, above all once you have learned that the night lays down cables that connect directly to dangerous gaps in the memory, cables along which fear travels like electricity. But the battles and the turmoil often lay below the surface, and a casual onlooker might have observed calm above all on those nights of standing guard against panic. Almost, you might say, peace of mind. A teapot on the stove, two men chatting in their slippers against a backdrop of gentle music, Satie's piano on *Après la Pluie*, say, or one of Brahms's violin or violoncello concertos, the books on the table, a glass holding paintbrushes and murky water, yawns after a certain hour, the record coming to an end, the smoke getting everywhere, the ice melting inside the tumbler to mark the passing of time and all its clinging drowsiness, the brimming ashtrays strategically placed within reach of our four hands, the cushions, the checkered blankets that clash with the upholstery on the couch, and finally, as if by magic, almost when you least expect it, the cleansing miracle of daybreak, the light dissolving the cobwebs of sleep in the nick of time, at the last gasp, not long before they were to begin their perilous transformation into something yet darker and denser.

Which is how things had almost always gone. However, the last time I heeded Jacobo's summons, his nerves were shot to pieces. His fear had a more solid feel than on previous evenings. This time he was afraid that someone—a man, a real human being—would attack him at any moment. He took great pains to make sure every door was locked and showed me, hidden behind the door, next to the entrance to his apartment, a baseball bat and a couple of axes he had gotten ahold of from somewhere or other and kept hidden so as to be able to defend himself properly when the time came. When I questioned him, he said that this was just in case, that there were plenty of scumbags out there, and that he felt safer this way. For a moment, I thought he was about to offer a more concrete explanation for that fear and that makeshift arsenal. I watched him hesitate over whether or not he ought to fill me in on a story of hatred and persecution that must have struck even him as beyond belief. No doubt he was afraid that I might have taken real fright on learning further details and would have had no wish to keep him company that night, and so he preferred to keep his lips sealed in the hope that I'd put such changes down to a worsening of his state of mind. Which is precisely what happened. I didn't wish to make any further comment, but at that moment it seemed to me that Jacobo was truly beginning to hit rock bottom. He couldn't concentrate on any reading that night and had no desire to put on any music, so as not to muffle the sound of footsteps on the staircase or landing. He doubled his usual dose of tranquilizers and spent most of the time peering out the window, all of the lights in the living room switched off, alert to every movement in the street, struggling like a guard on sentry duty to keep sleep at bay.

6

(a stroll)

The following day, on my evening stroll, I was struck out of the blue by a sudden thought: What if it turns out I'm seriously ill and the whole world is in on the secret except me? Just like that, as I cast my mind back over the previous weeks, I began to clearly see certain details that I had not fully grasped at the time: questions I had not quite understood, phone calls apropos of nothing, sideways glances as if of commiseration for no apparent reason. On the other hand, my shattered state was no great mystery to me—my pounding heart, my palpitations and, in general, the all-round toll that, for some time now, being alive had been taking on me. This became all too clear whenever I had to climb a few steps on any staircase. At the mere sight of an uphill slope in the distance, I'd begin to feel a shortness of breath, gasping for air like a fish on the sand. Meanwhile, the feeling that something inside of me was rotting away as I slept was a hard one to shake. I could sense my own skeleton as something increasingly green and watery, and the presence of a seaweed-like substance in my lungs. But the fact is I had spoken to no one. Might someone in my family have gotten their hands on the X-rays I leave lying around in envelopes here and there, or the test results that not even I could bring myself to look at? Had my siblings taken it upon themselves to consult one of my doctors? Had he informed them of something other than what he had told me? Did they phone one another every night to weigh up the options and debate the pros and cons of filling me in on the situation? Perhaps, right now, there are people agonizing over whether or not I ought to know, whether or not I would be plunged yet further into gloom, whether or not I would take the opportunity to settle some old score, or devote my days to squeezing every last drop from what little time I had left. Even I can't answer that. The idea of disappearing has always made me think of the sea at night, of a silence filled with black vessels. At times I think I would have no objection to slipping away if I could be sure of feeling nothing more than the murmur of my strength as it ebbs away, while breath abandons my body and fatigue slowly comes to rest, like a deadweight, on my various organs—my eyelids, my guts, my worn out muscles. But at others I start to doubt whether the suffering will cease after death or there will ever be any real end to this time of nerves and debris. In other words, though on paper I know that it cannot be any other way, at the same time I find it hard to believe that all this darkness, already so dense, can be healed by yet more darkness.

Seated at the terrace of a bar I tend to frequent most evenings, I linger awhile to eavesdrop on the group of women who were sitting at the next table when I arrived. This is by no means difficult, since they all but bellow at one another and act as if they were completely alone. The women are pushing fifty. Though a couple of them are a few years younger, their ugliness evens things out somewhat, otherwise they would have no right, or indeed any great desire, to be there. Most of them are wearing burgundy-colored tights, as if they had arranged it beforehand—out of a group of seven, four are sporting identical pairs. Others, the more daring members of this almost kamikaze commando unit, have opted for a leopard-skin design, their unruly thighs bulging out over the top of knee-high boots, the unmistakable, albeit unofficial, uniform of the divorcée venturing out on a Saturday night this Autumn/Winter season, broadcasting her right to revelry and proclaiming that she is still good enough to eat. They are waiting for the tardiest of their number to arrive. Typical, they say, who else? They criticize the woman with a certain amount of affection. They're on edge. For a moment they fear that she will ruin everything, and it would not, by all accounts, be the first time. They have a dinner date with "men," and this means that they are all aflutter, taking little mirrors out of their handbags every other minute, smoothing their eyebrows with their pinkies, or painstakingly touching up their eye shadow. They may well be cutthroat rivals a few minutes from now, but for the time being they still come to one another's aid, fussing with bangs and constantly telling one another how pretty they look. When they spy the group of men approaching from a distance, they rush to gather up their cosmetics cases, leaving only their cell phones, dry martinis, mojitos, and packs of Winstons on the table. It's been a long time since they last spoke of *boys*, and the very word *men* carries with it a vague hint of seriousness, dirtiness, and menace that attracts and repels them in equal measure. Men. Men always pick up the tab, they undress you with their eyes and see a body free of flab or scars, they drop you off at home in a car with white upholstered seats. By the looks of things, these guys are executives, men of a certain standing, not like the last night out. Much as the women have put their efforts into looking ravishing, the men strive to look sporty and laidback; ties are out this evening, they throttle the men quite enough as it is Monday through Friday. The most seasoned and forward of the women seize the opportunity to mark out their territory just seconds before the game gets underway for real. They let it be known at the last minute, leaving no time for any replies, for the men are now too close, that they have set their sights on this one or that one, on the tall, balding one, on the one in the deck shoes, though later—they know the drill—it will all depend on how things play out and any on-the-spot changes of plan will have to be duly relayed in front of the restroom mirror, where, as the dinner nears its end, when dessert is just about to be served, they will form a line and touch up their makeup. Another one, meanwhile, announces that she is here to eat dinner and that's that. She wants to make this quite clear, she insists, and she won't be dragged into anything this time. She knows full well what they're like, and, until she says otherwise, she's having none of it. She'll let them know if she has a change of heart; until then she'll hold firm to her intention of going home just as she came, all by her lonesome. Before you know it, another woman has allied herself with this wary stance—she's here for a fun evening out, end of story. That's the plan. Even so, just in case, they have each carefully picked out their underwear, they're freshly waxed, and they're even carrying little tubes of vaginal lubricant tucked away in their handbags. The scent of the heady mix of colognes with which they have daubed their wrists, necks, asses, groins, and even every last fleshy fold of what was once their waistline drifts over to my table. I feel the urge to make a quick getaway, for the whole thing is starting to make me feel a little queasy. I'm not sure quite why, but the scene also makes my heart sink. I think of the hours they've each spent at the hairdresser's that very morning, wearing a blue gown of the sort handed out in hospitals, seated beneath the hairdryer, their hair covered in pins, clips, and rollers. I picture them counting out the money left in their purses after settling the bill for it all—shampoo and set, eyebrows, highlights, fingernails and toenails— and I find the image oddly touching. I imagine them returning home in the early hours of morning, their feet aching, tired of forced grins. Their heads are swimming, and they've missed their favorite TV show. They have a run in their panty hose and a longing to break down in a flood of tears that, in the end, will not come, for the lure of tiredness is stronger still, and they fall asleep on the couch without fully removing their makeup, a bottle of fresh water and the ibuprofen within reach. That or worse still: waking up pinned under the weight of a hairy leg, sensing ragged breathing on the napes of their necks, and spotting on the bedside table, inches from their noses, a glass containing the false teeth of a stranger who a few short hours ago was dancing salsa like a maniac in the middle of the dance floor, his shirt unbuttoned at the neck, and telling an endless stream of jokes about black people and whores.

In a nearby park, I pause awhile to watch the old men who play boules every evening. I don't know if it's me or them, but it strikes me that they are bent double under the weight of a grief that should perhaps no longer be theirs to bear. As a general rule, a person now lives such a long time that he ends up shouldering much more than his fair share of sorrow, and this ends up taking its toll on his face. One consequence of the increased life span of those who live in the developed world, and one, moreover, to which little thought is given, is that unlike what tended to happen just decades ago, today's elderly are still around to witness the devastation wrought on the lives of their offspring, watching as they practically grow old, as they fail, as they lose the will to fight. Before, when death took these men, their sons were still strong, they had plans, beautiful wives, and a seemingly sunny future. These days, it is not uncommon for a grandfather to contemplate, before dying, the divorce of his grandson (he watches as the man pulls up a chair at the dining table in the family home on Sunday, penniless, his shirt wrinkled), whereas in times gone by that same grandson, for reasons of time, would never grow beyond the child who had to be picked up from school occasionally, his hand held on the way home, and who needed help with searching the street markets to find the soccer stickers missing from his collection. Nowadays, dying old men do not leave behind a world in motion brimming with plans and promise, as was once the case, but rather, more than ever, a valley of tears. That said, there is nevertheless a happy upside to this pitiful state of affairs: it is never so hard to turn your back on a desolate landscape as it is on one filled with the birds that Juan Ramón Jimenez claimed would stay, singing. What now lies ahead, more than the earth covering the coffin, is an endless Sunday evening, a haze of tedium and defeat. And it's easier to take your leave like that, for nothing lulls you to sleep quite like tiredness. It's no great sacrifice to leave the party when girls, drink, music, and strength are all long gone.

I walk away thinking of the number of worlds contained within the world, of how far and yet at the same time how close they are to one another, at once distant and huddled together. The combination of the tranquilizers and my afternoon stroll sometimes brings about a sort of reconciliation with the world that emerges in the form of a longing, a veritable thirst, for simple and gentle things. I think I've made a mess of almost everything in my life. In having gone too far, for instance, in the desire to fill my time, my head, my rooms, every wall, every shelf, spurred on by a strange *horror vacui* that in reality makes no sense. In short, I believe my past is overstuffed with things, and this is bad news as far as fear is concerned, for anxiety, by its very nature, is something that always returns, and because monsters rarely emerge from empty wells. Perhaps we set too much store by the urge, so symptomatic of the times we live in, to hoard experiences, a sort of Diogenes syndrome more of memories than of objects, and the trick to striking a certain degree of inner balance, if such a thing is possible without becoming a total cretin, may lie in blending in with the nothingness that surrounds us rather than rising up in rebellion and wishing to make of it a sort of giant, faceless foe against which to dig trenches and moats as if we ourselves were anything other than nothingness, as if we could ever truly amount to anything more than what remains, always what remains, what little remains, the almost nothing that remains after having traveled down a thousand roads, after having loved, after having lived between the devil and the deep blue sea, pinned against the sky and the rocks. As if we were anything other than skin that grows old, leaving a pile of ash and cold dregs sealed inside, next to our bones.

Our high school physics professor once told us that if an atom were the size of the Burgos cathedral, then its nucleus would be a pin on the floor, and its electrons, tiny specks of dust hovering beneath the domes. The rest would be empty. With this in mind, given that the world is made up of atoms, one might have said that everything was nothing. We ourselves were nothing. Though it might seem that objects bounce off one another, this is a simple matter of equilibriums and force fields, atomic orbitals, the hurly-burly of magnets in disarray. Any real contact is out of the question. Say, for the sake of argument, that I'm in love with a woman; what I actually love is a peculiar arrangement of nothing, a peculiar arrangement of nothing that bears her name, the form nothingness adopts in her, the way in which her millions of empty cathedrals interlock. I might think that I take her by the hand or caress her skin, but this can never be anything more than a sly trick played by a limited, sick perception. Truth be told, it is a game played only by air that is not even air.

No matter how hard I clutch her to me, what I hold in my arms, what I fear losing, what is killing me, is a whole heap of nothing.

On these strolls, I sit down for long rests on benches and take everything in very slowly—the people, the light, the evening itself. I buy bread for dinner, cigarettes, coffee, and anything that can be cooked in a pan, a minute on each side. Often, on the slightest pretext, I enter the Chinese dollar store two streets up from my apartment. On the closed-circuit TV, they keep an eye on me to make sure I'm not shoplifting. The store is run by this bleary guy who spends his whole time there, Sundays included, with the radio turned on and a handful of comics at his side. For a moment, I feel I could be happy behind the counter of that store, that I could hang around there for hours on end, my head empty of thoughts. I'd like to hang out there, with the young Chinese woman minding the shop while snuggled up to the electric heater, sometimes sewing or watching cartoons on a tiny TV set. I'd love to stay there all day long. If ever I made a big sale, I'd impatiently wait for one of the owners to drop by so I could tell them all about it, down to the last detail. I'd draw tally marks in pencil on a scrap of paper whenever I sold anything. At around three in the afternoon, someone would bring me a plastic container filled with rice and another with hunks of meat swimming in a different color sauce every day, and almonds, bamboo, and sprouts of one sort or another. I think I'd like that. I'd also like it if at the end of each day, the young Chinese woman and I counted out the coins in the till, and what little there was would strike us as plenty. Then I'd fall asleep at her side on a mattress on the floor, the East in my arms, as if at last I held distance in my grasp, surrounded by plastic odds and ends, cats with moving arms, huge fish tanks, and pictures with lights and waterfalls.

Some days I see this mentally handicapped guy stroll by. He must be almost twenty, and he's always accompanied by a woman who looks like she's his grandmother and buys him an edition of AS sports magazine, soccer sticker-album packs, and superhero comics. The two of them are pretty fat, and the kid is always dressed in an outdated Real Zaragoza tracksuit, the official design from four or five seasons back, beaming with pride. I figure that the boy is in his grandmother's care and that he barely sees his parents—it's been a long time since his father was in the mood to take any crap, and the man now spends his afternoons playing cards in a gloomy corner of some bar in the neighborhood of Las Fuentes, a tumbler of cognac and anisette on the next table, for his own table is taken up entirely by the baize playmat; meanwhile, she—the mother—who met a gentleman that seemed like an upstanding sort, runs a roadside bar three provinces further south where they also sell cheese, *mantecado* shortbreads, and melons. No doubt the kid attended school for a while, until they gave up on him as a hopeless case. He'd have had no one to play with in the recess yard, but would sometimes take refuge in his cell phone so as not to appear so forlorn. He'd pretend to receive messages, and though his classmates suspected he was making it all up, they'd have to prove it, because if you don't lose heart and you keep checking the screen again and again as if you hadn't a care in the world, a slight lingering doubt always remains.

81

Though I know the situation would be as foolish and as far-fetched as can be, I can't help thinking for a moment that I might be happy if I could be that kid's older brother or something, as ill-equipped as he is for life's struggles, also in the care of his grandmother, who would cook us hearty, humble stews every day, pots of macaroni and ground beef, and huge bacon sandwiches whenever snack time rolled around. We could share a room, which would be filled with posters of athletes and a smell of sweat that would, in time, cease to turn my stomach. He would show me his collections, the dog-eared albums in which no one until now had ever shown the slightest interest, his magazines, his badges, and we would stay up all hours chatting about signing rumors and zombies.

And if so much time hadn't gone by, if I had a little more energy and a youthful set of white teeth, I'd also like to be the boyfriend of some neighborhood hairdresser—let's call her Puri. Or Nati, Nati would do. I'd pick her up from work on afternoons of heavy rain, lingering awhile to chat with the other girls who are always chewing gum and discussing the articles in their magazines while they finish tidying everything to close up the shop, forming piles of hair of every color with their brooms. Perhaps one of them wouldn't mind giving me a quick shampoo while I wait. I'd like, moving the dream on a little, to have gotten married to her, to Nati, that is, to have acquitted myself well in the waltz in a restaurant in some industrial estate, filled with decorations and flowers and red drapes, and for the whole thing to have been caught on videotape, which we'd watch from time to time, when nothing on TV took our fancy—me cutting the cake, me teasing my new mother-in-law, fat and happy in her dress festooned with ribbons, the waiters refilling our glasses, Nati looking like a princess, her cleavage covered in glitter, or rather a fairy who's made all sorrow vanish without a trace, and the chanting crowd calling on me to kiss her, on the two of us to climb onto the table, to kiss each other again. Right now, this very afternoon, I'd get home, flake out on the couch, and rub my eyes so that she might ask me if I'm tired. Today, I think I'd tell her I've had a tough day. Yes, I'd tell her I've had a real tough day.

7

(they tell me he's dead)

The police called to tell me that Jacobo had been murdered. That night, his neighbors had heard strange cries and noises, and the next morning his buzzer and phone had gone unanswered. When the locksmith accompanying the police officers opened his door, they discovered his body lying prone in the hallway—in his underwear, which is the way he liked to wander around his apartment both summer and winter—riddled with knife wounds. When I hung up, I screwed my eyes tight to summon the tears, but it was no use. In the darkness of my heart, however, at that very moment, Celan again leapt into the river with a deafening noise, and everything was drenched by the water of the night. I thought back to the axes Jacobo had hidden next to the door the last night I went to keep him company, and I confirmed the suspicions I had harbored at the time that he was not then afraid simply of memories or nightmares but rather that he truly feared that a flesh-and-blood human being might attack him, as had sadly come to pass. This was not some worsening of the panicked state he had recently been struggling to keep at bay. Rather, as had now become clear, he had had more than sound reason to fear that a murderer might break into his apartment. According to the statements from the handful of witnesses who thought they had heard something odd, all this must have happened around about dinner time, at nine in the evening or thereabouts.

It would seem that my name took pride of place in the address book on his cell phone, next to those familiar words *in case of emergency*, which explains why the police called me ahead of anyone closer to him (on paper at least) so that I might put them in contact with his family, while gleaning the first clues as to his identity. I was touched by this tribute of sorts that Jacobo had paid me, now from the other side, by choosing me as the person to be notified should anything happen to him. On the one hand, he saw me as a guy who had his wits about him, someone capable, when the time came, of making decisions that might have been of a clinical nature and of vital importance, as if by singling me out he were announcing to the world, *This guy will know, when the chips are down, what has to be done.* At the same time, I couldn't help but take it as a humble, secret declaration of friendship, something along the lines of *I know that* you *care.* Yet I felt somehow guilty, for no sooner had I heard the news, right at that very instant, my thoughts were not for him, but rather for myself. Something like *great, just what I needed*—just what *I* needed. I don't know how far it's possible to mourn someone's death from any perspective other than one's own, by which I mean, the perspective of the gap left behind in my life and among my things. I'd have liked to have been able to mourn him, above all else, for his own sake, for the days he would now miss out on rather than for his absence from my days. I wanted to believe that he had lived his life to the full, that dreams, much like books, also count for something, and that fear itself, when all is said and done, is also life, that there is no need to travel down all the world's roads, to cram your life story full of incident and travel and love and persecution when the abyss forms part of your blood and your heart has been buffeted by every storm.

I believe they made the call from his apartment, their eyes perhaps on the corpse as they spoke to me, but I was not summoned to the precinct downtown until that evening. It's awkward having to field questions when your gaze has been obliterated, and it's all but impossible to keep a sufficiently clear head to be of any use to a detective at such times, when your hatred is directed at the whole world, indiscriminately, and at the turn events have taken—at that whole intricate, tangled mess of cause and effect that, to cut a long story short, we call fate. They wanted to know if he might have any debts. I didn't think so, I said. No, for sure, I said, and much less to the point of having to turn to some low-life loan shark or anything like that. They wanted to know if he might have any enemies. I told them that this struck me as impossible, for I was at that moment incapable of remembering anything other than his compassion, his home as if it were my home, that way he had of taking you in and hearing you out. On hearing the word *enemies*, my thoughts turned to those intangible creatures that inhabited the furrows of his brain's circumvolutions, the ghosts that ruthlessly hunted him down in packs, night after night, and against which he had so often sought the assistance of my mere presence.

But an enemy of that sort does not plunge a knife though the thorax. It does not kill like this. They wanted to hear about his way of life. Or *style*, perhaps they said *lifestyle*. You know, sir: customs, hobbies, habits, any detail might help. They looked at me as if I'd lost my senses when I told them he was a big fan of Samuel Beckett. I had no wish to make light of things at such a time, but my thoughts weren't flowing with any normality, either. Tripping over my tongue, I sketched a skin-deep, rough portrait of how I saw his life at that point: a retired man who devours books and DVD movies, something of a homebody, though he shops for his own groceries and goes out for strolls every now and then, as well as for the occasional evening meal, albeit much less since the ban on smoking in restaurants and bars had come in, forcing him to seek refuge in his apartment more often than not. He liked to complain that the disappearance of the smell of smoke in bars had only served to bring the smell of sweat, humanity, and armpits to the fore, and ever since, he had preferred to hole himself up with his wounded freedom beneath the reading lamp or in front of the plasma screen on which he liked to watch classic American movies from the forties and fifties, smoking to his heart's content, drinking whisky, going to bed when the mood took him, and getting up as and when he pleased. He would appear in the living room, yawning and stretching his limbs, rubbing his eyes but with a book already beneath one arm. A woman came by to help clean his apartment three mornings a week. I don't know if she had a key. Enemies? No idea. As for what he was up to, he told me plenty, but I don't know if he told me everything. I don't believe there's a person alive who doesn't keep a few things to themselves. Perhaps he was more apt to recount memories from long ago or events that took place only in his thoughts and less of what happened to him in the outside world or over the course of his day, but the fact is he was one of those people who live more in their memories than their own apartments. I know he had his sorrows, and also that he sometimes roared with laughter, that he was content dining on eggs and fried pork sausage and wine aplenty, or over post-prandial drinks with friends at the dinner parties they still throw once in a blue moon, wolfing down the cream on his Irish coffee by the spoonful; I know that he never entirely lost interest in the world or in women, though he was mindful that he was now surviving in the margins, off the path, albeit next to the path. The window next to his writing desk was like a watchtower from which to observe time as it set about grinding down the world, the passing of life, the clouds, the tedium. In a way, he was a little like old Cioran, whose adolescent readers took their own lives year after year while he, deep down a secret, shameful lover of life, jogged through the parks of Paris in his shiny track suit.

Back home, I couldn't help wondering how an outside observer might describe *my* lifestyle, or how *I* might come across to a police officer seated on the other side of a gray metallic table. Would what he heard make him envious? Would he feel sorry for me? No doubt it all comes down to who is doing the telling and how the tale is told, to the words chosen for the portrait. There are those who might say that I'm like a shadow roaming certain streets, always at the same hour, give or take, his hair unkempt, a scarf slung carelessly around his neck, slipping into bars and ordering coffee, barely speaking a word to a soul, and sometimes scribbling things down in a notebook or on any old napkin, on the bar itself, scowling and looking downcast in general, as if hauling a great weight from some ancient place, and whose apartment is no doubt gloomy and whose phone probably hardly ever rings. But from the outside, from a distance, I could also look like a man strolling at his leisure, his evenings free and the city all to himself, sometimes in the company of women who are by no means hard on the eyes, who hang on his every word and giggle foolishly at his wisecracks, who work together to make sure he doesn't let himself go altogether, forcing him out on the town and sitting him down in cafés, right in amongst them all, for a sort of therapy session, so they say half-jokingly. And, also half-jokingly, they chide him if they suspect he has returned to his old ways, shutting himself up in his apartment with his dreary books, without speaking to a soul even though the loneliness is killing him. "If I find out . . ." they say. "You'll have me to answer to . . ." And the odd one among them even appears to dream now and then of rescuing him once and for all from the helplessness he seems hell-bent on drawing attention to, almost as if unintentionally, with his three-day stubble, that constant look of not having gotten a proper night's sleep (if, that is, he ever actually made it to bed, which is taking a lot for granted), and his threadbare shirts, his long coats, and that way of walking of his, with a quick stride, just as soon gazing at the ground as at the tops of the plane trees, coming to an unexpected halt all of a sudden, absent-mindedly, in front of some store window, above all the windows of second-hand book stores, auction houses, and antique dealers, but also before the displays of furniture stores that project out onto the chilly street scenes of the life of warmth he always seems to be craving—lamps and pianos, porcelain dolls, toy racing cars, Japanese bedroom sets, reading corners with the light turned on, faded leather wing chairs that make you think of long winters, cups of coffee, trays of pastries, and piles of slightly dull books on the mantelpiece, next to the silver-framed portraits of ancestors. But all of that not just yet but rather thinking ahead to some vague future time, on the far side of the storm, after having lived just a little bit more, when he's given up for good and has finished doing battle with the tempests that now swirl through his thoughts and his heart says, "Here and no further," and he feels so weary, so sapped of strength, that he no longer wishes to hear of strolls or dingy dives or sneaking into buildings to probe the lives of others and dream awhile of other people's stories and hideouts and wives. That seems to be what he's playing at some-times, at manufacturing that image of neglect and helplessness that leads—whether by design or otherwise, who knows?—the occasional female friend to be seized by the urge to take him out shopping on an afternoon of sales and to give him a few tips on styles and sizes, what suits him and what doesn't, what's still in and what's out, and, in passing, to rearrange his closet a little, and even, while she's at it, to teach him three or four easy-to-cook recipes, dishes that give proper nourishment and can be whipped up in a moment and barely cost a dime, so that he doesn't carry on feeding himself any old way, as is his habit, with all that coffee, all that fried and refried bar fare, his routine in disarray. The neighbors would chip in with remarks along the lines of *you never know with him, sometimes three or four days will go by when you can't hear yourself think what with all the coming and going from his apartment at all hours, and other times a month will pass without hearing so much as a pin drop; sometimes you see him heading out, all dressed up in his blazer and expensive colognes, then that same evening you run into him on his way back in such a state that if you didn't know any better, you'd think he was one of those bums who sneak into the building to go begging for change from door to door.* More witnesses would then say their piece. The guy from the bar *La Canción* might add, *He'd been looking down in the dumps recently. Before, not so long ago, he'd turn up with two or three books he'd just bought, tearing the cellophane off with something bordering on delight, as if his mouth were watering. Then he'd leaf through them slowly, the index, the prologue, all that stuff, reading out random paragraphs here and there, scribbling something on the opening pages, the date and his signature, no doubt. He looked sad, true enough, but it wasn't the sort of sadness that debilitates you, rather it was as if he were somehow content there in his own world, immersed in his thoughts and those new books. A world away from the shadow that began to drop by later, his visits much fewer and further between, subdued and jittery at the same time, with a certain air of bitterness in his gestures.* Meanwhile, when questioned, my colleagues would no doubt point to my attitude of "not giving a shit." *Not rude, mind you, never altogether unpleasant, it's just that often you didn't dare talk to him, because it was as if you were about to wrench him violently back from some place deep down where he was happily submerged. But if you did have something to tell him and you finally plucked up the courage to do so, you soon realized it was no big deal. He'd*

91

even try to smile and pay attention to you, more or less. One of them, the lovely Araceli, might have more to add: *I don't think he was as antisocial as he might seem, there were times when I even thought he was about to come on to me at any moment, to ask me to join him for happy hour, as they call it these days, to grab a coffee one evening or suggest we catch a movie or whatever other excuse. I saw how he looked at my legs, I caught him several times looking at me longingly, you can tell these things, as if inwardly weighing up the goods and the cost, in other words, the meat and the price tag: on one side of the scales, the desire to rip my panties clean off, I think that was obvious, although maybe it went beyond that to include daydreams of another sort, more romantically inclined, so to speak, going for a stroll and not always being so alone and being able to tell me things; and, on the other side, myself as a millstone for then on, a more or less unavoidable date almost every evening, forcing him to emerge from his cave on weekends, the idea of his cell phone coming to life and my name on the little screen, of me as a deadweight hanging from his arm on Sundays in line at some movie theater or, worse still, in bars with music where there is nothing to look for because supposedly he's already found me. Though maybe this is all in my head, because the truth is he never actually said a word to me. It was just that way he had of looking at my legs, like I said, how he'd all of a sudden become lost in thought, and all those times he looked all set to say something only to bite his tongue.*

Nor was I left with any choice but to wonder whether or not *I* had any enemies; there has, needless to say, been no shortage of those who have wanted to kill me in the past, though I have always preferred to chalk that up to the madness of others or the uncontrollable outbursts that, in affairs of love and jealousy, I have always looked on as deserving a little leeway. Then there are those who come out with things such as *it's not that I wish him any harm, but I don't wish him well, either.* For the most part, those who make such statements would rub their hands in glee on learning of your death and would not hesitate an instant to cheerfully urinate on your corpse should the occasion present itself. Even so, I would not, strictly speaking, call them enemies. Having enemies is no simple matter, it's almost a tragic luxury and, depending on how you look at it, a gift from life as far as meaning and intensity are concerned. Which explains why so many people invent, imagine, or long for one. On the other hand, if I am apt to view the world as, on the whole, a hostile place, it is not too bold to think that the world (or part of it) might also, as is only fair, view me as equally hostile. I think, for example, of those who tried to approach me when I was at my lowest ebb and to whom I refused to pay the slightest heed, people who, based on a handful of traits, perhaps credited me with an outlook akin to their own, a certain type of sensibility, and who thought that I ought to have been thankful from the bottom of my heart for their outstretched hand rather than fleeing from them as if from the plague, those who attempted to strike up a profound nineteenth-century correspondence with me only to be met with a curt, tardy reply; I think of those women who, on seeing in me the living image of neglect, wanted to come to my rescue, to drag me out of the dark pits in which they imagined I spent my hours, without, in truth, ever scaling the heights of my desire—my desire for light or my desire for them—with their warm flesh and their smell of home; and finally, I think of all those whose fellow traveler I had no wish to be, whose warlike manifestos I returned unsigned, all those who sought to win me over to their cause, lost or otherwise, and have me march beneath some flag to the beat of their drum and not my own, and those whom I stood up, sooner rather than later, without bothering to offer the slightest explanation. But an enemy worth his salt must be hated above all in secret, when no one is looking, and I'd swear that, for better or worse, my life has been free of them. Thankfully, no one on whom I might wish to practice voodoo, no one I might picture, my eyes closed, being tortured and screaming on the rack.

They don't let you see the scene of the crime, but nobody takes the trouble to give the place a decent clean, either, and the bloodstains remain on the wall, untouched, a dreadful continent surrounded by brown islands on a vertical stucco sea. They must have scattered plenty of sawdust of the floor, for there were still lumps stuck to the baseboard on the day I decided to make use of the set of keys Jacobo had handed me some time previously and I made the decision to enter his apartment. About one week after the crime. At first glance, everything had been left more or less as I remembered it. His children and his ex-wife had dropped by no sooner had the police removed the seal from the door and business as usual had been declared on the landing. They took with them a couple of Pepe Cerdá paintings, said to be worth some cash, his old Underwood typewriter, which weighed half a ton and had been at one and the same time his emblem and his pride and joy (when this last fact dawned on me, I could not help but feel a twinge of resentment, for I had set my heart on that beauty, nor, at that precise moment, could I help but consider myself a wretched soul), as well as anything else of value they could find in the drawers following a quick skim through their contents: the gold watch he never wore, his collection of fountain pens, and not much else as far as I could tell, perhaps one or two of the bottles of wine left lying around, so temptingly, for all to see, though they didn't even have the good taste to choose the finest among them. They had told me over the phone that they'd be back soon, as soon as they could all coordinate their schedules a little, to see what was to be done with the books and all the rest, so that they could strip the apartment as quickly as possible, since it was rented, the meter was still running, and it wouldn't do to carry on paying month after month without rhyme or reason. In theory, the idea was to pack it all up in boxes and take it off to some temporary spot with enough room for it all, the house they owned in his hometown, no doubt, so as to sort through it all more calmly at some later date when they had the energy and some time on their hands. I pictured that heap of crates loaded on board a white van, heading for the country, before gathering dust in the woodshed of some ramshackle, cobweb-filled house, next to the farm tools, the rusty scythes, the foul-smelling clay pots, and the discarded wineskins, the tape sealing Jacobo's watercolor prints, his books, his love letters, his toy soldiers, a whole life packed away inside cardboard boxes and sprinkled liberally with rat poison.

8

(condolences)

The wake prior to the incineration was held in the rooms of the Torrero cemetery. If Jacobo's family had decided to bury his remains rather than burn them, they would have done so in his hometown. It matters not that he had made the decision some time ago to distance himself from that place and return to it as little as possible. This is a common state of affairs. As soon as someone has definitively lost any chance of making themselves heard or protesting, everyone else acts as they see fit. I've even seen sung masses, the choir packed with angelical children, to send off the most steadfast of nonbelievers, in the epicurean belief that death, like anything else, remains the preserve of the living. Perhaps it would not have been such a bad thing if Jacobo's remains had come to rest in the place he had spent so many years, no matter how often he had bad-mouthed the lovely Provincia and all its kindhearted folk who had fashioned a whole sophisticated system for whiling away their time out of snooping on others, speaking ill of their fellow men, and leaping to conclusions. It was, when all is said and done, for better or for worse, where his home was. And a home, an abode in the broadest sense of the word, need not always as a matter of course be the place where one lives, it can also stand for just the opposite, the place from which one is determined to beat a retreat, the little flag with a pin for a mast stuck into a point on the map, signaling, on the one hand, the place where, by dint of centuries and fate, the exact makeup of your own blood, blend after blend, has slowly been concocted, and on the other, the reference point thanks to which one can make a getaway, letting, as is only right, a little air, the rivers, and even, if possible, the sea currents come between you and it, to flee and never to go back; for even if you are never to return, you need a place to which you never return, precise coordinates that mark the spot on which you have decided to set up the ghostly camp of your absence, the chair on which you do not sit, the walls you do not hide behind, the steps you do not take, and the thousands of eyes that do not pin you to the spot.

Quite a throng had gathered in the corresponding room of the funeral parlor, for the most part people whom I knew Jacobo had despised with all his heart. Yet there they were, sobbing occasionally, inventing exploits and memories, embracing one another as and when they arrived, heading outdoors in pairs for a smoke. Whenever someone dies, a sort of public battle over grief breaks out immediately. Among the deceased's acquaintances, there are three or four who vie with one another to see who was his truest, closest friend and, by extension, who is most entitled to feel distraught and to be on the receiving end of the most heartfelt condolences. This contest is not always fought on the surface; one must follow it between the lines, in demeanors and conversations. The candidates focus their efforts on rebuffing and clamping down on any attempt to lighten the mood, frowning on all those feeble stabs at humor that are inevitably always made among those gathered together, as a way of letting off steam, seeking solace in the thought that the one who is no longer with us would have been a thousand times happier to see us laughing than to know we are this crestfallen, or something along those lines, or proposing a toast, sometimes even going so far as to perform the time-honored farce of filling a shot glass for him, amid nervous laughter and tears, before belting out his favorite song at the top of their lungs. The candidates refuse, under any circumstances, to play along, and will if they can prevent the rest from doing so, for it turns out that they, unlike the others, are grieving for real, and are in need of consoling, a little more attention, the heartfelt kisses of the others' girlfriends, if possible, and even for one of those girlfriends to refuse to leave them alone when night falls—you guys go ahead if you like.

Without ever saying so in quite so many words, the candidates' quarrel essentially comes down to two things, always the same two: how close they were to their lost friend and how recent and meaningful their last encounter was. This was what three of the frontrunners were squabbling over when I made my entrance in the room.

"It's unbelievable, not a week has passed since I last spoke with him."

"Four days, in my case."

"Two in mine. In fact it was he who called me. He needed to talk. He seemed, how can I put this, strange, and believe me, I know him well."

A civil war. The dead man being dead and therefore out of the running, for the spoils that go to the deceased are a prize that belongs to a different plane, the one singled out as his closest friend will for once take his place, before a far from sparse crowd, as the protagonist of something big, something serious and even solemn, and not without a certain degree of social cachet, no matter how fleeting. I'd have liked to wander over and tell them that their quarrels were unwarranted for I knew for a fact, based on plenty of conversations with Jacobo, that he had nothing but the deepest contempt for the three of them in equal measure, without further distinction, and that the absolute, utter indifference he felt toward each of them was matched only by that he felt for the other two.

I preferred to say nothing and to leave them there, cheerful in that crestfallen huddle, now all set to broach the time-honored chapter—which could well take the name "But How In God's Name Did We Fail To Notice"—in which their remarks had already moved on to the subject of how guilty each of them felt deep down, for perhaps they should never have allowed him to take off alone to Zaragoza under such circumstances, as despondent as he seemed, drinking more than ever (they lowered their voices at this point), his nerves shot to pieces, at war with the world. As if their opinions had ever counted for anything, as if there were ever the remotest possibility that Jacobo might at any stage have paid them the slightest heed. They say that, by all accounts, it was dreadful. They say that the whole house was filled with blood, that it must've been one of those gangs. They say he was a regular at the strip clubs, that he rubbed shoulders with underworld types, that he had racked up debts in almost every store on his street. They say that there's some bleached-blond Russian girl who's young enough to be his daughter. They say that that friend of his who came here with him did him no favors; we all know his sort, a dismal character if ever there was one, a regular ray of sunshine. They say that aside from the blood and all that, his apartment was a shithole—dust everywhere, the dirty dishes untouched, that goes without saying, the bucket where he put his dirty laundry filled to the brim and overflowing, smelling like a pirate's lair. Filth and rum. They say that he lived like an animal, the poor guy, that that's no way to live, although by all accounts he had his moments and he clearly sometimes realized the error of his ways, for he'd call people up in the early hours of morning, even his in-laws once in a while, only to fall silent, all you could hear was his heavy breathing on the other end of the line, before hanging up all of a sudden, without even bothering to pick up if his call was returned. They say that pride is a very bad thing, that no good can come of all that pride, that it was in fact that pride, more than anything else, that was his undoing, They say he took his medicine however he damn well pleased. They say all of that. They say he didn't even own an iron.

9

(alone on stage)

I'm not quite sure why I went to Jacobo's apartment or what I was looking for when I began to search his shelves and open all of the drawers, one by one. I pulled the door firmly shut behind me, donned his slippers, brewed some coffee, and got ready to stay there all afternoon long, taking my time, in the very place we had so often stayed up till dawn, discussing this, that, and the other. On my last visit, we had gotten bogged down in a conversation about the meaninglessness of it all, and he had asked me to change the subject, when, apropos of nothing in particular, we began riffing on the idea of the black infinity in which our planet floats, like a rudderless ship sailing on an ocean of anguish. He preferred more earthbound subjects and had lately been harking back to the past more than was usual in him, recounting the odd episode from his rural childhood—part picaresque, part nostalgia, and part horror—and his years spent at a Salesian boarding school, and his first brushes with love, which arrived without prior warning with all that hitherto unknown trembling, the first panic attack, an aching as incomprehensible as it was real, your skin torn off in strips by the love that has just savaged you minutes after the girl of your dreams first appeared on the scene like a carnivorous plant. The trap sprung by the pink dress, the ribbon in the hair, the gentleness that, when you least expect it, leaves your heart fraying at the edges and bearing tooth marks. Desire like a whiplash, the prie-dieu in the darkest corner of the chapel. The knees red and raw from all that kneeling and praying. The knees red and raw also from all those falls, from the thorny bushes on the flatland that looked from afar like a garden. We were discussing all this, somewhat in the abstract and without getting down to the specifics, the girls who plucked us from our childhoods without the slightest compassion, and the fear that hovered in the air, though always left unspoken, when the time came to take her hand in yours under an almond tree in bloom, and all that innocence that cuts through you like a rusty sword, the pale hands that daintily place in your chest, forevermore, a sorrow that is there to stay.

There was the battered leather armchair in which he liked to lounge and read and from which, just four days previously, he had held forth on Proust, waving airily with his glasses in one hand, and the yellow- and orange-hued checked blanket with which he covered his knees, and, on the side table, next to the ashtray still containing a fair few butts of his that no one had so far taken the trouble to empty, the pile of books he had been reading at the time: the two volumes published by Trotta of the complete works of Celan, *The Anatomy of Melancholy* by Robert Burton, the copy of Márai's *Diaries* that I had just returned to him and which had not yet been put back in its place,

L'espèce humaine by Robert Antelme, and a few notebooks containing his observations, sketches, and all manner of scribblings. He liked the two of us to read the same books more or less at the same time, for then he had someone with whom to discuss passages and exchange points of view.

Not long before, in that same room, he had been shocked by my theory that the difference between Auschwitz and military service of the sort that I did in Spain in the early eighties was merely quantitative and not qualitative. Immense, granted. Colossal, vast, there's no arguing with that, but merely quantitative all the same. That was my headstrong stance. Auschwitz was military service multiplied by a certain number, pick one as high as you like, but not a drastically different matter. I remember telling him that when humans who sleep en masse in barracks begin to move at the sound of a whistle, you're already halfway there. If I, at an intimate, almost physical level, can understand the testimonies of those who survived, even feeling an occasional, vague sense of déjà vu on reading the books of Antelme or Primo Levi, this is because I have on many a winter morning fallen into line in my underwear in front of the barracks and have mopped the floor of an immense building in which the bunk beds, the lice, and the boogers all blended into one. And because my head was all but shaven clean the minute I arrived, and because orders were barked at me to stand in the line for vaccinations and to stand in the line for the standard-issue attire and to stand in the line to have my bowl filled with soup and stewed meat, while all around me were watchtowers and spotlights trained on the tops of walls crowned with barbed wire and shards of jagged glass.

Needless to say, I was not claiming that having lived through all of that automatically entitled me to put myself in the concentration camp prisoners' shoes, but it did at least give me a firmer grasp on what they were talking about than could be said of someone who has never been ordered to place their thoughts and speech on hold, or paraded back and forth all morning long, or cleaned sardines and scrubbed toilets for hours on end. Without that experience of having been stripped of my dignity, I would have no way of knowing what it feels like to be on your knees in the mud, or to have your face trampled by a boot. Now, however, when I read those tales of the camps, I can picture the backdrop to all that ignominy, the guard's faces, the smell of muck and dirty laundry, and the depths of the envy you can feel toward any old dog of the sort that come to feed off the scraps from the trash cans left outside the back door to the kitchen.

And I was also trying, clumsily, to get across that other idea of mine, as old as it is muddled, that every human life contains within it the story of its century. Not, it goes without saying, in chronological terms, or in the form of parallels that can in any sufficiently clear-cut way be drawn. But I understood that those months back then, devoid of any hope, had been my Auschwitz, with their farewell to poetry and their sky teeming with vultures, with death hovering over everything at all hours and the lost beliefs and the broken banners. I told him that I could recognize in my own past the Jaca uprising, the face, the flesh of the woman who made me head outside into the snow to join Fermín Galán's men, singing, armed to the teeth, all the flags pointing straight toward defeat. And I also told him that on some good days, in the darkness of the barracks, I still held out hope of having my own Normandy landing, my May of '68, my time of burning cathedrals, and a Prague Spring that in my dreams took the form of a whitewashed patio filled with potted geraniums, not far from the sea.

Wearing his slippers, I lit one of his cigarettes and sat down to contemplate the living room from the position of his absence. On the other side of the window, at that hour of the afternoon, it seemed that the fears that had plagued him were still there, as if blind to the fact that their prey had already been struck down by another, more potent, force of nature. The clouds circled like crows as the natural light faded little by little from the room. This was for him the most dreaded moment of the day. The blinds shook gently in the breeze that at that time of day seems to come from the most bitterly cold nothingness. I turned on his stereo to listen to "Hurt," which had for me in recent months become something of a theme song for Jacobo in this little theater of ours. It seemed to me that Johnny Cash's voice was closer to tears than on previous occasions.

I then got down to the business of slowly searching his drawers, one by one. I was not looking for anything in particular, and at the same time I was looking for everything. I wanted to understand something. I wanted to let the objects shape my thoughts a little, guiding them, for otherwise, without the aid of those external prompts that at times conjured up precise instants, at others long stretches of time, my thoughts could not run freely. It's strange what the silence of a dead man's things has to say for itself and the way such objects have of keeping still. Some of them, a pair of glasses with an outdated prescription painstakingly preserved in their case, say, or an old wallet stuffed full of expired ID cards, appeared to have gotten a head start, surreptitiously and under their own steam, on their owner's death, for they had for some years now lain in the gloomy recesses of a wooden drawer, locked away and forgotten. Most of our things die before us, they said their goodbyes some time ago without our noticing. Others, meanwhile, those that outlive us, make no bones about the sudden interruption of everything— items of clothing with his sweat on them in the laundry basket, drinking glasses bearing the outline of lips now forever sealed, reminders of doctor's appointments he should have gone to the next week, prescriptions awaiting a trip to the pharmacy, tickets for a play that has yet to open in the city, an almanac on his writing desk with a whole ream of pages that now serve no purpose, and the hundreds of scraps of paper scattered here, there, and everywhere (Post-it notes on the refrigerator door, napkins from bars, dog-eared Moleskines) with snippets that could have amounted to something, who knows, perhaps poems or something of the sort, ideas for an article, fragments of letters that went nowhere.

I needed to understand something, to get some inkling of who might have killed him and why, and as things stood, I had nothing, other than the certainty that he had feared this attack and that the police had ruled out the motive of robbery. When I arrived at Jacobo's apartment, I had Lorazepam coming out of my ears. Though that state of extreme sedation didn't exactly help me get my thoughts in any proper order, I felt sure it was the only way to face the ordeal of entering his apartment alone, of seeing the blood stains on the wall, and of finding myself among his things once more. Even so, I gave a start at the slightest noise from the upstairs apartment or the inner patio. It's impossible not to feel like an intruder when rooting though the pockets of a dead man's coat, rummaging around in his nooks and crannies, reading all his papers.

10

(one day the investigators will come)

I returned home in something of a daze, without having
gotten a single thing straight in my mind. I thought it
would be best to go back another day when my thoughts
were a little less cluttered and I had some idea of which way
to turn or where to begin, anything other than turning up
and grabbing some object, then caressing it awhile before
putting it back where I'd found it, which was more or less
all I'd done the entire afternoon. I opened the front door
to find my apartment particularly silent, and as if tainted by
a half-sickly light, of the sort that leaves everything tinged
with ennui. In my listless state and as if spurred on by a
strange inertia, as if the detective work I had undertaken
in Jacobo's apartment just moments before had somehow
carried over, I began to see my own possessions as if they
belonged to someone else, in other words, as if I were in
some way dead, or worse, and someone had wandered
in and begun to survey my things, the mess, the furniture,
the books, in a bid to find something out about who I was
and what my undoing had been, the ultimate reasons for

the disaster, for my aimless drifting and my empty hands, for the shadows that cut through me, and all the rest besides. In one of those folders I hadn't opened in decades, I came across a handful of letters sent to me a long time ago, most still inside their original envelopes, as well as the odd draft of others penned by me, which I must have set aside at the time in order to keep a copy, to what end I no longer know. I picked one at random, addressed to the first girl who ever truly got under my skin, back in my high school days. The first thing that struck me was how little I remembered of her. While I could clearly recall a pair of her dresses and could sketch the door to her apartment block on the Calle Costa Rica, her face was much harder to summon.

Dear Magdalena,

They told me that I'd forget you, that all this pain would little by little ease and that a few years from now I'd again be able to stroll calmly down the streets I roamed with you and again enter the bars in which we got drunk together, and even sit down again in our usual corner at the end of the bar, under the same darkness as back then and that music that enveloped us, without panicking at the sudden emergence of a memory that might again bring back the taste of punch on your tongue or the image of my hands creeping up your thighs, of your raised skirt and your moist panties on the bar stool.

They told me that's what always happens. That the sorrow passes like a mountain storm and gives way to other suns and other skies, taking with it the pitch-black sea of clouds that roared before up on high like the sky of Golgotha over the wooden crosses on which flesh hung, now dead. They told me that my life would carry on and that things would happen in the future and that there

would be more travel and women and also more desire, why not,
and that one day, almost without my realizing it, a time would
come when I would once again sleep the whole night through, I'd
see, and that I'd again eat at mealtimes and would be able to get
by without the hundreds of pills in my silver case, without having
to drink on an empty stomach, without clawing at my skull, and
that I'd no longer feel the desire to make bloody tracks on my arms
and hands with a box cutter.

They told me all of that. But time goes by and my love will
not leave. I loved you so much, you bitch, that my love cannot
leave. It's here to stay. And it hurts. And it remains. And it will
not leave. It has made its nest in me, like a snake holding out
come hell or high water among the throbbing rubble of my ruin,
and sometimes it rears its head with its forked tongue, with its
bloodshot eyes, and it waits for you like before at the entrance to
the movie theaters and looks for you in bars and down alleyways,
and, asleep or awake, it dreams only of reaching you wherever you
may be to bite your heart. And there it remains. It does not tire.
And it hurts. And it will not leave.

I don't know what arbitrary, strange force it is that
sometimes keeps me from tearing up this type of letter
while other times it compels me to do so there and then,
filled with rage. Shame comes into it, needless to say, that
much I do know, but the underlying reasons are beyond me.
My initial instinct, no sooner had I read the letter, was to
destroy it, but even as I was thinking of doing so, my fingers,
as if they had a life of their own, were neatly folding it in
two and putting it back in its place. On other occasions,
in similar situations, just the opposite had occurred: while
my mind was all made up to safeguard some piece of paper

as if my life depended on it, my hands were suddenly crumpling it into a ball before setting it on fire inside the sink. On this occasion I kept the letter, as if I might one day reread it or need it at some future point as documentary proof of something—quite what is anyone's guess—on some sort of eventual day of reckoning. It's as if everything in a man's life is leading up to a settling of scores with himself, at the gates to oblivion, that in the end never actually takes place. When not thwarted by the surprise arrival of death, it is prevented by all the weariness that tends to precede it, ruling out any attempt at a reckoning or stock-taking with its *what does it matter now* and its *we tried our best*. Or by shame itself, for in truth there is no such thing as a life that when looked at in hindsight and with a little perspective is not, deep down, a source of shame, even the lives of heroes and martyrs. Starting with the life of Jesus Christ, then the rest of us from there on down. It's enough to make you stick your head in a hole in the ground, ostrich-style, never to emerge again.

My hands behind my back, as if sleepwalking, I scanned the shelves—the spines of the books, the objects that keep them partially hidden from view, little boxes, figures, framed photographs, and the wooden shelves themselves, all with their very fine coating of dust. For some strange reason, it seemed wrong to move anything, as if I were standing before a museum exhibit or the scene of a crime. It was as if the final whistle had been blown on some game and to touch anything, much less move it from where it stood, would now be cheating. I knew that my life was there, or at least the keys to my life, if indeed my life has ever had any keys, coordinates in the shadows, or has ever obeyed anything other than chaos, improvisation, or happenstance of the purest sort.

Written on the opening pages of each book is the date on which I bought it. Many also feature the name of the city, while a few also contain an additional note on some circumstance or other of that day: who I was with, if the book had been bought as a gift, if I had stolen it and how, if it was raining heavily. And some, albeit the exceptions, even contain within their covers the occasional surprise of some sort that also speaks to the time in which they were read: a dedication from an ex-girlfriend in that sweet handwriting that ex-girlfriends have, a faded movie ticket, a subway pass, some dried petals flattened between the pages. Assuming that anyone might ever have the necessary curiosity and time and were willing to take the trouble, all my books could be arranged in the precise order in which I had purchased them, almost down to the day, and based on that sequence, it would no doubt be possible to come up with a theory about rather more than my changing interests and taste in books: my urges to take flight, my obsessions, my soul, in short, or at least my soul as I liked to see it at each stage of my life. And if, to stretch the point a little further, that timeline was then set against the events of my life, a parallel biography, as if beneath the surface, would then emerge and might perhaps explain a great deal about the events that unfurled up above and shed some sort of light on my actions, my getaways, my terrors, my infatuations, my moves, and all that followed in their wake. Which book lay on my bedside table the night I felt sure I was dying of love for the very first time, aged sixteen, the night I covered my pillow in snot and scraps of poetry?

What was I reading when I was abandoned in an interior apartment on the Calle Bravo Murillo, whose hallways then filled up with deathly music, cat shit, and beer bottle tops lined up on the floor along the baseboard of the entire length of the hallway? What book did I have on me when death gorged itself on what I held most dear and turned the whole world, with its streets and its seas, into an endless tomb beneath the cover of a sky that became for me like the inside of the lid, upholstered in blue, of a giant coffin? The contents of each and every book mingles with those of my thoughts at each moment, and it might not be too bold to claim that they must have influenced my decisions somehow, or at least the moods that inspired such decisions. My mind has been filled with those words, tangled up amongst them, tainted by that ink whose marks formed, deep down, mental images, sometimes hazy and sometimes crystal clear, distant worlds, outlandish characters, lies and battles, women as if glimpsed through a trellis of blackened wood, prodigious tales, hospitals and jungles, wonder and bile, the human heart with all of its ravages, and the blood that seeps out, boiling or ice cold. It's impossible not to see those books as part of who I have been, allies and culprits in equal measure, for better or for worse.

I've arranged the volumes of fiction by their original language, then in more or less chronological order. Works of philosophy and non-fiction have their own bookcases and rooms. A library spreads out like an infection or a monster unfurling ever more numerous, longer tentacles. Then there are a series of special shelves in favored spots that at some point I began to call altars, devoted to a particular author or subject matter, with their corresponding ornaments and illustrative photos. These tributes have changed over the years. Now, for instance, there is an altar to Marguerite Duras, with the various editions of her books, besides which I decided to place those of Robert Antelme and Yann Andréa (who else?), so that she's not altogether on her lonesome, as well as a bottle of Bordeaux that must be vinegar by now, deluxe editions of her movies *Hiroshima Mon Amour* and *India Song*, a bookmark bearing a picture of her seated, *Emmanuelle*-style, on a rocking chair, and a collection of postcards, with their black cardboard case and red ribbon, published by Les Éditions de Minuit and featuring the photographs that Hélène Bamberger took of her and her things, and of Yann, and of the sea, in the outskirts of Trouville in the early eighties, her face so lined with wrinkles, her terrifying thirst for peace of mind, her thirst, period. This is but one small example. The books by Mexicans are joined on the shelves by bottles of tequila, of the half-sized sort usually picked up at the airport right before boarding the flight home, and small potted cacti that call to mind a scorpion-filled desert, while the most tropical part of the library has been set aside for those by Rudyard Kipling, right where the leaves of the pothos cascade from on high like a green waterfall. It's impossible to take out one of his books without first having to brush the branches to one side like the native guides of explorers. Sometimes, as can be seen, the combinations of books and objects reflect the most hackneyed of clichés (scenes of *milonga* and the *mate* with its corresponding *bombilla* straw next to the Argentine stories, miniature ships and antique compasses

flanking Stevenson and Conrad, a leather-bound hip flask
next to those of Malcolm Lowry), but sometimes they can
be put down to more secret, intimate associations of ideas
that would leave any casual observer utterly baffled.
Things of mine, objects that only I know belong there
and there alone. That's where I should focus my attention.
If there is some key that might help shed a little light
on things, it is no doubt to be found there, mixed up in
amongst the secret threads that bind the furthest recesses of
my mind to that section of the library.

And then there are the shelves housing movies and
music, which also endeavor, more or less intentionally, to
tell a life story. Almost every movie I ever saw in the art-
house theaters on Sundays back in an age that now looks
golden from my current decrepit state is there. Whether or
not I actually liked those movies at the time, whether or not
I ever even understood them, is neither here nor there; pick
up a program from Cinestudio Griffith or El Regio from the
early eighties, scan the titles, and you'll discover that every
movie, every single one, is on my shelves, see for yourself.
And the same can be said for the singers who left their mark
on moments of my life, the concerts that truly set my pulse
racing, the songs that for a time became private anthems,
for they seemed to speak about me or to understand me in
a way that was beyond the humans that surrounded me. It's
all there, albeit jumbled in amongst other records I've barely
listened to, though I thought I would when I bought them,
perhaps because I harbored the secret intention of beginning,
one day, to be someone else.

Surveying my shelves now, it seems to me that they
bear witness to the story of a fraud and that they might

at most bear witness to the depths of a being who doesn't actually exist. I think that those crammed shelves speak less to who I am than to who I wanted to be. It strikes me that every collector, be they a consummate bibliophile or a teenager looking to assemble the complete output of their favorite band, has in mind, albeit in an ill-defined, generic, or prototypical sense, the idea of a visit that will one day be paid by an individual they have not yet met, someone to whom they will reveal that treasure trove of items gathered together over the years, not without a great deal of hardship and penny-pinching, (or, better still, who will see it for themselves, without the need to have it pointed out to them, and who will spring up from the couch in one single bound to take a closer look), and who will know how to appreciate it and will be able to spot there and then, thanks to all that stuff, the sense of a whole life, the identity of a man. Every library, no matter how personal, is arranged as if on display. It seeks out the other, it craves admiration, the simple recognition of a like-minded soul or a polar opposite. This is not altogether uncalculating, for it is, when all is said and done, a language. And as such, it may be heartfelt or duplicitous. One would first of all have to know, in each case, who is being addressed, who, for each of us, that blurry silhouette might be, that mysterious caller, always as unexpected as death itself, who will turn up one day and take final stock of our things, and will know who we are by tallying up what is here and what is missing, volumes and gaps, treasures and absences. For if not, then how come it's impossible to get a wink of sleep if but a single volume is not where it should be and, in an enormous living room, crammed full of belongings, furniture, and volumes, the first thing that leaps out is the gap left behind by the book that isn't there, the one, say, that was lent out and has yet to be returned? And there's no need for a physical space to actually exist, since books have a way of huddling up next to one another, and doubling up, and lying sideways, filling the space up to the next shelf; the simple knowledge that that missing spine, with its color, its exact words, ought to be standing between another two books is enough to ensure your gaze is always drawn to that spot. The fraud I spoke of earlier lies in the fact that my library might not, as I have always thought, be the map of my soul. Yet it remains to be seen who I was hoping to fool, whether more or less mindful of this fact, over the course of so many years. Sometimes, when I give the matter some thought, I picture a woman, well into the early hours of morning, a glass in her hand, browsing my shelves. She wears her hair tied up and removes her raincoat to reveal a black dress that leaves her bare shoulders on display. She takes out a book now and then, leafs through it, then puts it back where she found it. She has her back to me and pays me no heed directly, though I wander over to her every now and then and softly kiss her back or the nape of her neck. I make the occasional remark on what she is looking at, but she doesn't listen, she has no interest in anything I might now have to tell her. She searches for me among the spines of the books she lightly brushes with her fingers. She searches for me there and there alone. Which might explain why, without fully realizing it, I have spent my whole life working up to this future moment or this delirium of which I occasionally glimpse a faint image, with piano music and the rain beating down on the other side of the window. Other times, however, I think that the one who's been duped is none other than myself, a more innocent, trusting side of me that revels in it all and takes comfort in the belief that he has managed to make something of his life, that he has built something.

It struck me that my dead friend's apartment had made me look afresh at my own home. As if I had already begun leaving everything at the sole mercy of absence. The door firmly locked, the electricity cut off at the mains, the dust spreading out at its own pace, so like that of eternity, over all the silence of lifeless objects.

One day the investigators will come. They will search the apartment, suddenly emptying out the contents of upturned drawers on a table. They will unfold papers, poring over every photograph, every letter, newspaper clippings and bank statements and receipts for my most recent purchases. They will hold in their hands the objects that were first ours, back when you still dusted them down from time to time with a feather duster (your headscarf, your song . . .), and then belonged to me and me alone, so mournfully, while all of a sudden becoming smaller and a little older, and that will from here on in belong to no one, fodder destined for the trash can or trinkets sold by the pound in the best case scenario—the multicolored dragon souvenir we bought in the Park Güell, the teapot from Fez, the half-rusted box of quince jelly from Puente Genil in which you kept the postcards we still received from time to time in those days, the sailboat with cracked masts, the miniature Chicago taxi cab. In their notebooks, they will jot down the words they deem important, almost everything, in fact, just in case; things turn up when you least expect it—what I thought on one day only, what I wrote without realizing, the date scribbled on the back of some theater program or movie ticket, the clues to a life, the half-erased traces of footsteps heading straight for an abyss without anyone yet being able to understand why.

One day the investigators will come. They will rush through the letters I took such time to write, the unfinished stories, the poems still full of crossings-out and minced words, cringe-worthy verses, coy observations. Their eyes will flit at great speed over the adjectives I pondered with care, their clumsy, latex-gloved fingers will in the end cause the ink to smudge, small blue clouds with traces of fingerprints slowly forming in the middle of the sheet of paper. One day the investigators will come, and they will discover what I never knew, the hidden reasons for my fears, the source of the storms, the night's motives, they will know why I did what I did when I did it and will train their microscopes on the ice that at other times brought me to a standstill; they will barge their way into the forests I had no wish to roam and upturn the sacred, the delicate, the half-broken, everything that held itself upright as if by miracle. One day the investigators will come, and they will know who I loved.

11

(the boy among the pigeons)

In a cardboard box, I come across a black-and-white snapshot of myself cutting through some pigeons in a square, probably the Plaza del Pilar in Zaragoza, though it's such a close-up image it might well be the Plaza Cataluña, in Barcelona. Whatever. I must be around four or five; I've never been much good at gauging children's ages. It's winter, judging from the coat I'm wearing buttoned up to the neck, though my legs, as was customary at that time, in my family, at least, were exposed to the elements no matter how cold it got. Either way, I can clearly recall that coat, which was in fact red, with its Eskimo hood, while the argyle socks and the badly buckled shoes also strike me as oddly familiar. Yet I cannot fully get my head around the fact that that boy is me. The word *me* blurs in and out of focus, I'm not sure I understand it. The sight of that boy arouses in me a tenderness I find hard to sustain. I look at that boy and my heart goes out to him.

Child, forgive me for all the harm I've inflicted on you, for what I have ended up making of your life.

Forgive me for not having listened to you more, little Rocamadour of my own novel, little cardboard horse, for not having spent more time with you. I look at this photo, and for the first time in my life, I feel I can truly see you. You are not only me, by which I mean, you are me, but you depart from within me, you slip free of the filthy jail cell of my limited identity and become a child, pure and simple, out there, deserving of every tenderness, lots of love, even this love of mine that is now poor and a little drab and has a way of sometimes tainting things whether I like it or not. If I could see you entirely from the outside, I would want to protect you, to kiss you; no harm could come to you while I was nearby. I'm not sure why good sense tells me I cannot harbor such feelings simply because you are me when I was small, I cannot fathom today this strange shyness I ought to feel when loving you and all of a sudden no longer feel, perhaps because I am already sliding down a ramp that leads who knows where, to the middle of some stormy sea or dreadful silence. I look at you and I know I could learn to love you like no other. For no other living soul could I have done as much as I could have for you, living as I have lived within your skin, my hand on the tiller, on paper at least, guiding the steps you take in those patent-leather shoes with a buckle on one side that now seem somewhat comical. I could have watched over you like a Guardian Angel, defending your laughter and your innocence and the four corners of every bed you ever had; and yet I have ruined the life of no other creature as I have yours. You look a lot like one of my sons when he was your age. You are all but identical. I would have laid down my life for him and still would, yet to you I have left barely a thing: these black lungs, if anything, wretched loves and nights of terror, a liver on its last legs, a few friends, but always the same noose slung hovering so closely over your throat and all this weight with which I saddled you. I look at my knees today, my hands, and it takes some effort to believe they are the same as the ones in the photo, the same eyes, the same legs that once held you upright. I can barely believe I'm still alive. In other words, I know that I'm still alive but don't understand it.

I feel the need today to tell you that I loved you in my own way, even without knowing how to. That I like the fact that you're my past, and that I'm proud of your high school diplomas and the things you sketched with a few strokes of a pen on any old scrap of paper, some of which I still keep in an old folder at the back of a closet, monsters and mountains with clouds up on high, ice-cream vans, racing cars of every color, soccer players poised to strike, revolvers, and princes on horseback.

I don't know the point at which I let you die. In truth, I'm not even sure you're really dead, altogether dead, I mean, but even so, allow me to say how truly sorry I am if that's how it was, if I was unable to hold you tight enough when you left, when you slipped away from me to who knows where. Your skin was so smooth, your dreams so crystal clear. Now that I can no longer hear you, now that it's been quite some time since I last felt your heart beating within me, in the darkness in me, I want you to know that the place in my insides where you once slept clutching tightly to your plastic truck, with your toy elephant, your hand-me-down pajamas, your longing to get to know me just as you thought I'd turn out to be and in the end did not know how to be, aches from the sheer cold.

If you had had your way, I was going to have coal-black, lustrous hair and would almost always be sporting a crisply ironed white shirt, that much I do remember, though I'd also have another one of the type worn by explorers, perhaps bearing the odd badge of honor of the sort kings bestow on men of action. And a pair of thigh-high boots. And sunglasses. I was going to have a big, bright-red convertible and would forever be heading home, very tanned, from journeys to islands and jungles no one had ever heard of. There are a ton of postcards that in the end you and I never sent anyone from anywhere. I sometimes think of those postcards, of their astonishing skies. As things turned out, no one back in Spain ever fought to collect the exotic stamps they would bear with hard-to-remember names of countries, with *W*s and *H*s in them, and each one a different color and size. I guess nothing ever came of all that envy we hoped to arouse in the world, taking photos of ourselves grinning and sporting all manner of hats by West Indian ports and atop the peaks of Asia, of all the native languages we were going to learn to speak, the arts of fishing and war, of the mysterious ebony masks that were going to adorn the walls of our apartment, filled also with treasure chests found in temples buried beneath blankets of ivy, and amulets to ward off bad luck, and jewels, and daggers we would sometimes show to visitors, taking great care so as not to break them. I'm afraid that the white shirt was about as far as we got.

I can't even ask you not to forget me, for, thankfully, a child cannot remember what will become of him. Which is why they—children—laugh and play, why they do not leap from the cliff tops. But I do ask that you take me at my word on a few things: it was not my wish to distance myself from you, I remember you on many days, almost every one; I would have liked for us to spend more time together.

12

(lion's cage)

The first weekend after Jacobo's death, it was my turn to
be with my children. And it was by no means easy, first and
foremost as I did not want them to notice the state I was
in, and time and again I found myself with no choice but
to head outdoors so as to be able to cry out of eyeshot. I'm
taking out the trash, I'd tell them, or I'm off to buy a loaf of
bread, I'm going for a stroll around the block to get a little
air. Only to break down in sobs at the first corner I could
find where I figured no one could see me. I looked for
doorways left ajar, entrances to garages in which to weep. If
I drifted too far from home, I'd have to race back, as, for no
reason whatsoever, I'd get it into my head that something
dreadful might have occurred in my absence, no matter
how brief it had been—a cracked skull, a gas leak, another
map of blood on the wall or the tiled floor. I'd picture one
of my sons, his head resting on the chest of my other son's
dead body, weeping and calling out my name. Weeping of
the sort I'd only ever seen in the movies, his mouth open,
his entire face drenched with tears. Then they'd swap

roles. If at first it was my eldest lying motionless on the floor, the figures then flipped around, just like in those old schoolyard scuffles in which, locked in an embrace, we would literally roll on top of one another across the earth, and this time the corpse was that of my younger son. My hands were shaking so much it was all I could do to fit the key inside the lock, and when at last I managed to get the door open, I would see before me the most domestic and peaceful of scenes. I'd sink into the couch to catch my breath, but my beating heart took hundreds of minutes to settle. Not that the infernal racket of the PlayStation did much to help, with its endless battles between Martians or zombies, its shrill music, and its planets in flames. I had to tell them I was sick to see if they might take a little pity on me and also so that they wouldn't be altogether taken aback when I set a place only for them at mealtimes, while I sat at the other side of the room, without touching a morsel, or paced from one end of the apartment to the other like a caged beast.

Something had rotted away inside my head, thoughts that broke off from their course and began to fester on the shore. I couldn't stop myself from penning letters in my head. The words flowed, sometimes out loud. I'd forget the beginning and start afresh. Dear Jacobo, for example, dear Jacobo, now you are dead, it's all over, the books you left lying half-read on the bedside table and on the bookshelves and here, there, and everywhere, the romantic trysts you had set in motion or harbored in the filthy bedroom of your imagination, and also the unease on those nights when you could not bring yourself to be alone. You will never hold a grandchild in your arms, you will not return to Proust in that future, ideal winter you had in mind, with snow and vintage cognac and a lit fire next to the enormous window you sometimes sketched. Nor will you ever make good on that fantasy of yours of sending out, on some birthday or other, for a handful of whores of the most expensive sort, as you liked to put it, of the type that dress up as Parisian ladies at the drop of a hat and speak several languages and have a certain poise (and, indeed, *savoir faire*) wherever they might find themselves and who wear on their person the most authentic silk, brought from China or wherever, and who feign desire as only they know how and part their lips in that way they have and then it's game over, for they have been trained to act as if they would drop dead there and then should anyone prize them away from your flesh. Dear Jacobo, now you are dead, and I am sitting in your apartment, in near darkness, while a few blocks from here, at my place, no one is waiting up for me. Dear Jacobo, now you are dead, I ought to be thinking about who killed you, and yet I think only about who might kill me. And that makes me feel like scum. That and the fact that I was unable to cry when they told me the news, not even the following day at the cemetery. Only now, somewhat too late in the day and perhaps thinking more of what the loss means to me than the end, in and of itself, of your being. It occurs to me to call you up and ask to borrow those axes, and also so that this time it might be you who comes to keep me company at my place at night, for I can feel how the fear is growing within me, and I don't know which way to turn when the past returns, where to hide, because I turn off the lights and shut the doors but the blood will not rest or sleep or be silent. Then it dawns on me that you truly have gone, and it's as if it were happening all over again, small aftershocks of your death in my head. I thought of you as the maddest of the mad when I discovered that primitive, makeshift arsenal half-hidden in the entrance to your apartment, I thought that you had already veered over the edge and were a prime candidate for the psychiatric ward, at which I'd have to visit you on Sunday afternoons bearing chocolates and cartons of cigarettes. And yet you have been proven, in the worst possible way, to have had good reason to stay up all night long, on guard and armed. It turns out that the threat was perfectly real and not the fantasy of a sick man with sweaty dreams of bloodstained blades, much as he might just as well have filled his thoughts with other, no less dreadful things, like the horror of the planets floating in the darkness of infinity and filling everything with a vertigo and a solitude too vast even for the universe to hold, or the possibility of dying at short notice without knowing any love other than that which has already come and gone, that recollection as sweet as it is hazy and that barely lives on in the memory as something that was ultimately tossed away with the trash, that was used up unwittingly in a time long since passed that was one of plenty, or at least appeared to be, when we would return from the supermarket laden with diapers and economy-sized packs of condoms and provisions too plentiful to fit inside the fridge and everything was as it should be and life was like the heavenward journey on a freshly painted swing in a garden dotted with olive trees. Before the light began to fade and the blood drained from everyone's lips.

Dear Jacobo, you've been murdered and I'm thinking about my life. And this hurts, for it has not escaped my attention that it is selfish, when all is said and done, much like when you would try to get things off your chest and I'd simply bide my time, waiting for the chance to butt in and get things off mine. The thing is, even seeing it so clearly, I cannot stop myself so easily. You went mad, and with your soundness of mind, hand in hand, mine, too, evaporated. You are dead, and what I feel, at every turn, as clear as daylight, under my skin and in all of the air that surrounds me, is my own death. I am powerless to stop it; if my thoughts were not so free, so elusive to my own will, I would no doubt have been a different person, I'd have been happy. And it so happens that these days I've also been thinking back to the words Robert Antelme wrote his friend Mascolo in a letter: "Dionys, I should like to say to you that I don't think of friendship as a positive thing, I mean as a value; much more than this, I think of it as a state, an identification, therefore as a multiplication of death, a multiplication of questioning." I remember that you made me read *The War* and all that we spoke of back then. And though, out of modesty, we were unable to meet one another's gaze when uttering certain words, I believe we were well aware of the space that anguish occupies in every love. Now you have gone and in some way you're dragging me behind you, you take with you on your departure the meaning of things, as a lure so that I might race behind you, so that, sniffing after that bait in tireless pursuit, I might end up lying by your side on the same drab beach on which one breathes one's last, seagulls shriek, and songs fade out. Yet there is nothing to reproach or even lament—with due conviction I shoulder the weight of a single cross that is mine to bear.

Allow me also to say one more thing. Some years ago, your death would have been a thousand times better, when you still lived with a woman who loved you. There was a time when you'd have said your goodbyes to the world with the sense of taking your leave filled with love. I've seen it elsewhere, in relatives or friends accompanied to the very end by wives who fight with the doctors, who move heaven and earth to get one more test, a painkiller, or a bed next to a window overlooking the pine forest, ones who stay in the hospital all night long, night after night, without so much as opening a book, simply saying goodbye to you with their eyes, making you feel that the journey that is coming to an end was a thing of wonder and that, somehow, it was all worth it. Setting metaphysical or biological considerations to one side, death is something that has to do with absence, an absence that must be noticed by someone. Those of us who live as alone as lepers cannot die in this sense, for we have in a way already been dead for some time. To truly die, you must leave a gap behind, the place at the table where you sat down to have breakfast with the others and where no one now pulls up a chair. Death is that bit of the table on which a cup of coffee is missing. You must leave behind an empty chair if you wish to die a proper death or for anyone to remember you some day; and, Jacobo, the empty chairs you leave behind you go unseen, they stand in a lonely, locked apartment. Which is perhaps why I feel that your death belongs to me, that you died only for me, much as I, had things happened the other way around, would have died for you alone. And if any light is to be shed by your end, if any lesson might be drawn from all this, there can be no pupil other than myself in the empty classroom at whose lectern you all of a sudden fall silent as I watch you for the last time from the only desk.

I return from searching your apartment in the early hours of morning and then continue with the search of mine without pausing, throwing myself yet further into the task, as if among my things, as outlandish at it might seem, some of the answers to all of this might be found. And I forget about you. And I search my own bookshelves, the backs of my own drawers. I open dusty folders filled with old papers, with one corner folded down, that I can no longer identify. My military service ID and high school diploma even appeared from somewhere or other. I take another long hard look, one by one, at the photos I have for so long been reluctant to face, in search this time of some clue, retracing the steps of a life I have for some time now been unable to understand. Or that I have perhaps never truly understood but that now, for some reason that has to do with a padded coffin, absurdly upholstered in tulles and velvet, in which you lie, stitched up from head to toe like a rag doll, I need to understand in one way or another. It may not always be the case, but sometimes death (and I believe its imminence, proximity, or even a simple hint of it may suffice) illuminates everything. And it is precisely beneath that light when it becomes clear that there is nothing to see.

Cotton buds were placed in your nostrils and earholes, and some elderly women, aunts of yours if I understood correctly, drifted away from the window in which you were on display, commenting to one another that you were more handsome now than the last time they dropped by your apartment some months back to make sure you were coping. Less bloated, they say, what a difference, and as if more at peace, as different as night and day, without those wrinkled bags under the eyes that could make one shudder. Look, Jacobo, I don't know much about detectives or police investigations. That's never been my strong point. Even as a reader of fiction, as you well know, I've always had more of a French, melancholic bent, just as you liked to tease me about; I've always preferred an interior monologue over convoluted stories that unfold amid revolvers, bona fide clues and red herrings, enigmas and alibis. I almost always lose my bearings. I never fully understood *The Big Sleep* or *L.A. Confidential*, whether in book or movie form, to cite just a couple of examples of the ones we've discussed a thousand times. But one thing I will say despite it all, right now, here, in the midst of the silence spreading out from your casket and now strangling my throat: I am going to use every last living drop of what little remains hidden among the debris of my intelligence, no matter how ill it may seem, no matter how feeble, to make sure that it simply doesn't end like this.

13

(still waters)

Things being as they were, and with the growing sense that everything around me was coming apart at the seams, I headed off to visit my mother at the old folks' home in a bid to cross at least one item off the burgeoning list of minor regrets and unfinished business that has a habit of getting in the way of thought and even life when it grows too long for comfort. I'm not always able to visit my mother, and sometimes the simple fact is that I cannot summon up the energy. I'm not sure the extent to which she knows who I am any more, but there's no doubt she's pleased to see me. At least she looks proud whenever it's her name, and not that of any of her fellow residents, that blares out on the megaphone that announces visitors from the scores of loudspeakers distributed along the hallways, and everyone, residents and nurses alike, the crazy and the sound of mind, busies themselves trying to find her in the rooms or among the hedges lining the garden paths. She feels important, which is why she always makes her appearance beaming triumphantly at all of her fellow inmates to whom no one has paid a visit that day as she makes her way to the room in which we sit. She proudly shows off her box of chocolates, her bottle of perfume. She shows me off. Some of the women remark on how tall I am, what a fine specimen I am. They ask my mother how many children I have, if I'm the eldest, if I live in Barcelona, questions she cannot answer. She answers yes to each one in turn and laughs happily, clinging tightly to my arm. For that alone, my visit is worthwhile.

I sit there watching her. It's true, as everyone says, that we look alike, but even more so when she's frightened. Then, we're all but identical. The large bags under her eyes are the same ones I contemplate every morning in the bathroom mirror, a little more wrinkled, perhaps, but just as deep. It's like a reflection of my own ruin, only grotesquely amplified, a bit like a verdict that this whole debacle of mine could be a lot worse than it already is and that the particular process of demolition in which I'm immersed continues unabated. It's enough to let time go unhurriedly about its business. For the moment, I recognize the anguish in which she loses herself as my own, I can sometimes feel myself tumbling down slopes that are in her head, into wells that belong to her. With her walking stick, she roams these corridors that always smell of stale soup and used diapers, and she does so with my own weariness, much as I stagger through my days under the weight of hers on the other side of the ivy-covered walls. In my bones I can feel the weight she bears on her back, and I even sometimes walk on her aching legs, almost always rummaging around, just like her, among sunken memories. I think of my current confused state and these nerves writhing on top of one another within me as the small outpost of a dementia that belongs to her.

I know she's going to tell me the same old stories. There hasn't been much variety to her repertoire lately. Things from way back, from a time long since passed. I take a deep breath and resolve to be patient and to try and listen to those tales as if I were hearing them for the very first time. Sometimes she recounts them as a memory, and sometimes it's as if we were still in the midst of that time. She takes me back to the streets of her childhood, which smell of wood and soapy water trickling down the gutters along the edge of the sidewalk, and once again tells me how she and her friends, in the games they played back then, liked to sneak into the houses in which a wake was being held, spurred on by a morbid dare. In the entrance to every house there stood a table covered in a black cloth, a book of condolences, and a silver platter bearing cards, one corner folded over as a token of mourning. The girls would climb the stairs, trembling on the inside, acting prim and proper and truly downcast until they reached the right floor. The door was always ajar. They might grab a cookie or two as they passed through the room, or a handful of sugar cubes, and as soon as they'd seen the body, they would sprint down the stairs, half-hysterical, doubled up with a laughter that was anything but light-hearted. They would never let a chance pass them by, and whenever they spotted the macabre signs in a doorway, a new game would begin in which none of the girls could be left behind. The game was cut short once and for all one winter afternoon on the Calle Padre Huesca when they discovered that the dead body lying on the bed belonged to a child their age.

She still describes the scene as if she were seeing it now, the boy's face so pale it was almost white, how dry his lips looked, the short trousers, the rosary beads in the clutches of stiff fingers with the cleanest, most neatly trimmed fingernails she had seen in her life. I think that what she's getting at when she tells me all this is that, quite simply, one day her childhood came to an end for good, and it might well have been precisely that day.

One thing then leads to another, and she inevitably moves on to another of her old favorites: the Easter procession the year in which one of her classmates headed out with the brotherhood performing the Seven Words while brandishing a banner bearing the words *I'm thirsty*, and how that same classmate, just days later, drowned in the river, and what folks said, wavering between terror and jest, and the fear of laughter, and sorrow, for back then the incense that filled the air was still a smoke that arrived dense from the world of shadows, sent forth by a wrathful God who, though it might appear otherwise, took note of everything and sometime forgave and sometimes did not. This was during the same period when she was banned from taking to the streets to join the Procession of the Holy Burial during Holy Week, owing to the public disorder caused by the scenes of terror and the bloodcurdling screams from the balconies, the uproar and the charging throngs on the sidewalks, born of the popular belief, very firmly entrenched, that wherever the sinister float came to a halt to let the bearers catch their breath, someone would die that year. And she described to me the blade of that rusty scythe in the clutches of the skeleton vanquished and trampled underfoot by the angel, the scent of melted wax, the sparks that flew when the Romans' spears scraped against the cobbled streets, the wailing of children, and the bare feet of the hooded penitents, their eyes deep behind the slits in the cloth like hidden, menacing animals, their black leather gloves, their bloodied ankles, the chains they dragged behind them as they walked. And the fear. Though she spoke to me of a time in which I had yet to be born, it was as if she were refreshing memories of my own, for the fact is I, too, have seen all of that, except for the famed Procession of the Angel of Death. My mother would not have us miss the Easter processions for anything in the world, which leads me to think that she considered that all that cowering, that fear she felt as a young girl perched on the edge of the Calle del Coso with her little bag of lupini beans, would in the long run do her children some good, almost as if she wished to offer us her very own nightmares, something about which she could later console us, thus making us more alike, bringing us closer together and causing us to need, just as she had begun to some years previously, to leave the light on in the hallway in order to be able to sleep. What she was looking to give us was a certain idea of intensity, much as when she told us bedtime tales of terror and abandonment. She was equipping us with all of the darkness we were unable to see with our own eyes and which, by contrast, made us appreciate all the more the daylight, the everyday household objects, the hours of tedium, the bowls of soup, the homework notebooks, the scent of soap on sheets and pillows, her own scent as she leant over our beds, just before switching off the light, to wish us goodnight, one by one, and sketch an invisible cross with her thumb on our foreheads. One cannot truly love a safe haven unless there are dark forces lurking outside, a world brimful of orphanages and tombs and beasts, of children who have gone hungry that night and a wind that howls as it whips around the corners in neighborhoods in which we had never set foot.

I listen to my mother talk, seated in front of her coffee, with those girlish gestures and her gaze lost in the distance, and I picture her mind as existing within a ravaged landscape—fallen trees, dried-up ravines, houses torn down. I think of those twin panoramic images on the news showing the same view of a city before and after an air raid: on the left, a cathedral tower topped with bells and storks, and on the right, the heap of rubble that lay in its place; on one side, the sturdy bridges over some river anywhere on the map of Europe, and on the other, the solitary pillars protruding from the water's surface like concrete stumps. Then I turn my gaze on myself and wonder if, after a certain age, the mind can be anything other than a ravaged stage—raised floorboards, nails jutting out here, there, and everywhere, stripped wires, spotlights that shine no more— and if there is nothing for it but to place there, half in darkness, everything we see or that happens to us, so that it might blend in with our existing memories, the desolation of before, the ancient fear. Once you have a few years on the clock, this new form of a priori sensitivity to the outside world emerges sooner or later—the broken stage of a two-bit theater in ruins on which the world unfolds, now moth-eaten, with no show to premiere, poorly lit. That's where everything must go, good and bad. Outside those borders lies the dark realm of the noumenon where, owing to its sheer vastness, there is room for nothing, nothing happens, and nothing has a name.

She asks me to take her to the cemetery. She makes the same request of everyone who happens by, including visiting strangers, the waitresses from the cafeteria, and the other residents. Without much success, but this does nothing to stop her trying. I lie to her once again: I don't have my car, I took it to the garage to be fixed, I had to come to see her by bus. She tells me that when no one is looking, neither the old women nor the nurses, she pulls up flowers from the garden to leave on my father's grave, but they always wilt, hidden at the back of the closet, since no one wants to take her to the cemetery.

It dawns on me that everything we've discussed has to do with death. Dead children laid out for viewings on postwar afternoons, drownings in the river, Dad, people fleeing amid screams from the shadow cast by a plaster angel. When I take my leave, I make the sign of the cross on her forehead just as she used to when saying goodnight. She smiles.

All of a sudden she is a child loved by someone. I think that when she dies and her brains mingle with the earth, all that most belongs to her, that is most hers—in other words, the damp crevices of her brain, say, or the wells of anguish, the entire labyrinth of blood vessels through which her fears stumble without reason—will live on in me. I know such things will stay here. Easy now, Mom, I tell her, soon you'll be dead but you'll be able to breathe. And we'll carry on sharing whatever is left, the nothingness of us both—the air I drink in up on the surface, its tedium and sorrow, will be for the two of us, as will the darkness in which you lie.

14

(password)

Deep down, though I had no wish to stop and think about it, I knew from the beginning that all that searching inside Jacobo's apartment, rummaging through his things and his papers, listening to his records, and looking over and over again at the half dozen photos found at the back of a drawer, had less to do with efficiency than it did with poetry, and that these days the keys to untangling a person's comings and goings, as not only investigators but also any child with his wits halfway about him will tell you, are in fact to be found on his computer. It is there, together with his cell phone records, that all traces remain.

When the police handed back those devices, the corresponding card was missing from Jacobo's cell phone, now little more than an empty shell without any data to comb through other than the date and the time. His computer, however, appeared to have come to no harm and was largely untouched. I imagine they'd have kept ahold of a copy of the hard drive in order to search for any strange goings-on using his browser history, but the fact remains that they returned it in one piece, leaving me free to spend a good few hours snooping around in the folders and checking out the websites he had clicked on recently— plenty of Wikipedia, plenty of articles on art, literary blogs, and that sort of thing, but nothing that caught my eye in particular in terms of finding out if he had gotten himself mixed up in any funny business. He had not, in recent months at least, visited any hookup or marketplace sites. Nor did he frequent gambling sites. He didn't even have online banking. Compared to my computer, not that I get much use out of it, you could say that his laptop was all but empty. Absolutely nothing of what he had saved on that appliance held any interest whatsoever, save, perhaps, for a few photos he had of a woman I had never seen before who had gleaming, golden thighs, the color of roast chicken. The photos were stored in a folder he'd named "N." In one of them, she was striking a pose, squatting on her haunches as she buckled her sandals and smiled for the camera. In another she had her back fully turned as she whipped up something in the kitchen, while in the rest, all taken on the same day, judging from her clothes and hairstyle, she was facing the camera in various spots of what looked to be a neighborhood park like any other. In each one she appeared alone. Entirely domestic images, not cropped or retouched, and somewhat poorly framed. It did not look remotely as if they had been downloaded from anywhere or belonged to an actress or anything of the sort. One look at those photos was enough to know that something powerful had existed between that woman and my friend. It was one of those things you pick up on at a glance, in barely an instant, without anyone being able to put their finger on quite why. Something so powerful, moreover, that it could perfectly well be confused with a distant recollection of love, or worse besides, and which might explain why Jacobo had had no wish to talk about her to me, as he had spoken of so many others he had thought of as passing fancies, in order to shield her name from the onslaught of my fantasies.

I looked long and hard at that woman. She struck me as foreign in many ways. Foreign to the country, sure, but also to time, to morals, to the world of things and gray streets I had lately been calling home, to the point where it seemed almost inconceivable that the two of us were breathing the same air. I zoomed in as close as possible on the image. Looking at her eyes, I thought that I would like one day to see a sorrow for me reflected in them. I pictured her seated on my deathbed, taking care of me, raising a glass of water to my lips. For an instant, albeit a split, almost imperceptible second, I was glad that Jacobo was dead.

I had to do whatever it took to get my hands on the password to Jacobo's email account. If there was anything that might shed a little light on things, it would no doubt be found there. For starters, I tried out one he had typed in my presence some time previously and that I had unwittingly committed to memory, but that one no longer worked. I knew, for he had told me himself, that because of his forgetfulness, he liked to have a short password he could use for everything. Among the dozens of items lying on his desk, all stained with ash, I spotted a yellow Post-it note, its adhesive strip now faded, on which he had written the word *barcarole* in his small handwriting. As soon as I set eyes on that random word written down there, without looking as if it belonged to a medicine or anything like that, and uncapitalized, I knew I had just found what I was looking for.

In the folders containing sent and received messages, it turned out that N stood for Nadia. They had not exchanged many letters. Right from the start, they must have switched to the telephone as their standard means of communication, perhaps so as not to leave behind any traces of the sort I was sniffing after. In any event, it was clear that, quite unlike Jacobo, Nadia was a woman of few words and did not feel entirely at home setting her thoughts down in writing. The first message, from him to her, dated back some eight months previously:

Nadia, you'll have noticed the clumsy, last-minute way in which I asked you for your telephone number and this email address to which I'm writing, and the foolishness of my excuse will not have escaped your attention: we both know that there are a thousand different ways to get your hands on the books I agreed to lend you. They're everywhere. Everyone has a copy. Perhaps they've even formed part of your collection for years now, and at this very moment you can see their spines from your chair as you read my email, and it may also be, in fact it would not surprise me in the slightest, that it is I who does not have them, or indeed ever did. I couldn't take my eyes off you at dinner, but you know that already. At this point I can only hope that our fellow diners, your friends in particular, didn't pick up on the fact that I didn't give a damn about the others or their conversations. No doubt you noticed that I've been around the block a few times. I'm a guy with a past, as the saying goes, not that that makes it any easier to write a letter of this sort. For this is a letter, is it not? Much as it might reach you across mysterious airwaves and through all that jumble of cables and sockets. I always tremble when faced with love. Do not be afraid of the word I use. It's for want of a better one with which to understand each other, though it might not be altogether inappropriate when I think of how you've occupied my thoughts since the night of the dinner, of how I made my way home whistling in happiness and terror at one and the same time. But fear not, though I might now offer you my entire life, without a thought for how appealing or not such a gift might be, there's no denying that it doesn't amount to much in terms of quantity. At a certain age, to offer one's life barely amounts to a thing. Let me rephrase, if I may: I always tremble when faced with a story that is beginning, as much when I was a schoolboy knee-high to a grasshopper as tonight while writing to you, now old, with hairy knuckles and glasses without which I'd barely be able to see beyond the tip of my nose, operated on a thousand times, half-rotten on the inside. I tremble above all when, as now, the matter is at that stage in which, on paper at least, it could still be all or nothing, when I might end up handing you what remains of my desire and my time from here on in until the curtail falls, or I might never see you again. Without, naturally, turning my nose up at any of the marvelous alternatives that lie somewhere in between, which involve you dropping by my apartment once in a while to listen to music, just like that, lying down on this very couch on which your presence is now missed, letting me undress you. But the fact is that there is a coin in midair, it's been falling in slow motion for days now, and that's what makes me tremble and implore who knows what gods not to let it fall on the side that condemns me to simply dreaming of you.

I have seen Jacobo put a great deal more effort into letters of this sort. There was a time when he'd show me almost every one, and there's no doubt that, in comparison, this one was a slovenly, half-hearted attempt. It struck me as odd that he made no mention of the inner world that could sometimes be glimpsed in her gaze, a golden oldie if ever there was one, or of how he believed he had caught sight in those stormy depths of the reasons he needed to carry on breathing, of the challenge of making up for a past brimful of hurt and of scheming. It took Nadia four days to reply, and she finally did so in a handful of lines that I reread several times between glances at her photo.

You're crazy, completely crazy. The thing is, I've been giving this whole matter some thought for a few days now, and I think I want to see you. Placing the dreadful fear I feel and that you cannot understand right now on one side of the scales, and, on the other side, the disgust I feel toward my life the way it is right now, I think I do, I want to see you. But do me a favor and forget all of that bullshit about love right now, that much I can tell you. I think we could be happy with just paying lip service to it, rolling around nearby it. Don't even think about calling me. Let me call you. I'll call when I can find the words. More words, I mean, apart from these ones that are just to tell you to wait for me.

The following messages came in the wake of a first meeting between the two of them that must have been a beautiful, heady encounter. I realize we are talking about a perfect stranger. I realize we are talking about a friend who had died just days before, his body still warm in its grave, as the saying goes. It matters little; though there's no accounting for any of this, what I felt was a lot like jealousy.

II. NO ONE

No one kisses like the desperate.

Manuel Vilas

15

(nadia)

It wasn't long before I wrote to Nadia. In my head I drafted
email after email, how many I couldn't say. I'd head out for
a stroll and I'd be writing to her. I'd duck into a bar to grab a
coffee and I'd be writing to her. I'd be watching a movie
and writing to her at the same time, letting myself be swept
along in a frenzy of words. Also in my head I tore up sheet
after sheet of paper before kicking them to one side. Then
I'd start afresh. Dear Nadia. Esteemed Nadia. Just the name
Nadia and nothing else. You don't know me. I'm a friend of
Jacobo's. I'm not sure how to tell you this. I don't know if
you've heard the news of his death. He was murdered, in
fact. If you did know, then you'll know how dreadful it was.
If you're finding out now, if these words are the first you've
heard, I'd like you to imagine them accompanied by a warm
embrace for you. I'd like to see you. I don't understand a
thing. I'd like to see you so that we can talk.

She called me that very night. I was lying on the
couch and eating a pizza while watching a documentary
about double agents during the Second World War when

the phone rang. It was a minute or two after midnight. I turned down the volume on the TV, and Nadia's voice reached me over a backdrop of black-and-white images of soldiers striding through the snow. It's me, she said. She did not identify herself with her name. She simply said *it's me*, as if there were no way I might be expecting any other call. As if she were my wife or something. She did not, as I had imagined, have a Russian accent. In fact, she had no accent at all, and she spoke very softly, as if she were afraid of waking someone. It was one of those rather catlike voices, with a natural inclination toward whispering that make you rue the fact that you are not on sufficiently intimate terms to change the subject all of a sudden and come out with the sort of lovey-dovey drivel spouted by lovers who live far apart and who call each other every day after dinner, without much to say, their hands toying with the buttons on their pants. I told her how events had unfolded, what little I knew, in reality, while the TV screen showed bombs falling from the skies of London and Dresden and columns of prisoners taken on the Russian front and marched semi-barefoot toward the trucks, their eyebrows white from the frost. Nadia could barely get a word out. She stuttered a little, and her silences were so lengthy it sometimes seemed to me as if the line had gone dead. I had no wish to lie to her about how I had come across her name. After thanking me again for the information in a somewhat stilted, almost inaudible fashion, she seemed in a hurry to hang up. Though she made no protest in that moment, it was clear that she did not like the idea of a stranger reading her letters one bit. Without much conviction, she began to outline a farewell that I was in no mood to hear. The unusual circumstances in which we were talking for the first time, the brutality of the murder, and all the rest besides freed me from any need to stand on ceremony, so I came straight out and asked her who she was. Who are you, Nadia? Where did you come from? The TV was now showing how by applying a special product with a paintbrush, messages written by spies in invisible ink would appear. And also how much information can fit inside a single typewritten period when looked at later under a microscope, everything you need to know about the enemy's plans in less than one square millimeter. Somewhat half-heartedly, Nadia began to explain how she and Jacobo had met, the "friendly" relationship they'd had, making light of the matter—a meal, the odd stroll here and there, three or four conversations, in some of which my name had cropped up. There were cardboard dummy planes and tanks at the Pas De Calais in an attempt to throw the Germans off the scent and keep them away from the Normandy coast. Nothing was what it seemed, let alone what it claimed to be, as I listened to Nadia's voice on the other end of the line. Her breathing was the biggest giveaway, the alarm in her voice. I want to see you, Nadia. I want to see you, now that the Spanish troops are all set to cross the Oder and Stalin is bellowing from high up on a balcony draped in flags, now that Eva Braun, in the heart of the Alps, is shooting a full-color film of her nieces showing off their new dresses, playing with a ball and smiling for the camera. I want to see you, now that the diggers are beginning to unearth the dead bodies at Auschwitz and the snow is starting to melt in Leningrad. I want you to tell me what's

151

going on here, I want to see those thighs in the photo up close, to reach out and touch them, I want you to come wearing that same dress, with your Greek sandals, I want to hear what the tremor in your voice sounds like in person and to see if it has anything worth listening to in the midst of these nights that are shackled to one another, each one strangled by its own chain, because you know what? I'm on my own now, and I'm pretty drunk tonight, and I'm speaking to you from an apartment that festers in darkness at all hours, no matter whether I turn on every light and fling the windows wide open, for it's as if the darkness is born beneath the beds, right where the dead bodies would sleep in your childhood and you'd look and it seemed there was nothing there, but they were there, all right, and they burst forth now, so late in the day, and the darkness that springs forth from down there below then clings to the walls, and is oily, too, and it sticks to the fingers and to the mirror and fills everything with shadows and cannot be removed with detergents of any type or gusts of wind or any music whatsoever, an apartment in which everything right now is upside down, upturned drawers emptied onto the dining room table, books that might or might not burn in the bathtub, I haven't decided yet, albums and notebooks piled up on the floor, ready for the day when I can bring myself to look at them, to turn the pages without closing my eyes or looking away. Come, for Berlin is now a vast expanse of smoldering ruins, the survivors make their way through the rubble, their eyes glazed over, and everyone is looking for bread and counting the dead, Nadia, you who hold between your legs the key to the secret, the meaning of the meaninglessness, and all the light I'd like to drink tonight. A dead man who slipped through the same hole through which I'd say my life is ebbing away as we speak, as I munch on a now cold pizza and watch as the Jews, their heads bowed, march toward the gas chamber, and everything is sinking, now and at the same time in the past, into the same mud, outside time, and I'm talking to you and you're telling me nothing. I came away with the promise of a meeting the following day. A coffee. It's astonishing how long it's been since I last wondered what to wear tomorrow. That delightful problem—which shirt, which jacket, sunglasses or no sunglasses, what pair of shoes to carry me to wherever she might be.

16

(perhaps love is not the word)

Some of the mechanisms that Nadia's voice, more than her conversation in and of itself, triggered inside me, together with the painstaking search I was conducting of my own apartment at that time, with all of the papers, forgotten objects, and old photos that turned up in drawers and folders and the most unlikely of nooks and crannies, made my thoughts turn more than might be desirable to the presence of love over the course of my life, in general terms, you might say, and to whether it might be possible to come up with some sort of story of that presence over time, whether there might be a sort of thread on which to pull that might, following a pattern, somehow bind together the collection of triumphs and wounds, or if it all came down, at most, to disjointed episodes, more or less blurry in the memory, like out-of-focus images or snatches of songs without an overriding melody that might bestow on them something akin to a meaning. I have a stack of letters in different handwriting bound together with one of those hair bands, a strip of photos from a photo booth, now all but faded to nothing, showing me and Laura horsing around and pulling faces before kissing each other solemnly for posterity, various hats at the top of my closet, single-use bottles of shampoo stolen from hotels with something scribbled on the label (those middle-of-the-night check-ins, trying to keep the stiff cock beneath your pants hidden from view behind the counter and the girl two paces behind, her eyes on the floor), scraps of paper bearing messages left for me over time on a host of bedside tables, from promises of eternity to notes saying "be right back," a little box made from what I guess might be mother-of-pearl in which I keep two rings, a green plastic one that was given to me one night beneath a vast moon in Berlin Park when I was fifteen years old, and a gold wedding band with a name and a date engraved on the inside (if I look long and hard at that word and those numbers, there comes a point when their meaning all of a sudden evaporates and all I can see is the material, pure and simple, the grooves once etched onto the metal by a small machine). I have a ton of stuff that may or may not be connected in some way, I'm not sure, nor do I know if the pain it causes me to touch them is of the same kind. I think of the faces I have held in my hands, caressing a cheek with my thumb, and of how eyes and lips now blend into one, when my battered memory brings forth from parted lips the wrong taste or a tongue that should not be there.

On Sundays, a thousand years ago now, I had to attend mass with my siblings and parents. When we went in the morning, we'd head to the Church of the Salesian Brothers of Francisco Rodriguez, and if, as tended to be the case, we ended up putting it off until the evening, then we'd have to make our way, for scheduling reasons, to the parish of San Antonio on the Calle Bravo Murillo, up near the Alvarado subway stop. This was, above all in winter, the saddest moment of the entire week. Though I was still too young and what the grown-ups liked to call those awkward teenage years were still a long way off, throughout the entire ceremony, I could not stop staring at the women's legs. I couldn't tear my eyes away and took particular pleasure in observing them from behind. The stitching in their panty hose, the shape their high-heeled shoes gave their calves. Panty hose of the nude, black, and sheer varieties. I also liked it when they knelt down in unison at the sound of the bell that gave the command from the altar, and when they gently beat their cleavages, saying, "Through my most grievous fault," there, flanked by rows of lit candles, the gloved hands, the shawls, the breviaries, that whole mixture of perfumes. I dreamt that they'd stand still for me, that they'd get to their knees at the urging of my command, too. And I fantasized, too, about a sort of magic spell that would pin them to the spot, while my parents were blinded and time came to a standstill. Everyone, myself excepted, as if frozen inside the church. Which was when I'd wander over to a few of them, the ones I'd picked out beforehand, undoing a button here and there, all very slowly, running the tips of my fingers over their lips. I'd touch their hair and, I think, their knees. But it was not long before such caresses struck me as lacking, too meager for a dream in which nothing is out of bounds, in which anything goes, with time stopped in its tracks and the whole world blind. I'd grab a large kitchen knife and plunge it into their calves, in a down-

156

ward, almost vertical, motion. But they did not stir or fully awake in the mental performance I staged—it did not hurt them, they made no attempt to flee, they did not scream. I was frightened by such a powerful yearning to watch as the blood ran down their legs, becoming trapped in every angle of their mesh tights, all that softness stained with the red of painted lips or of the sign on a whorehouse. Perhaps love was not the word, but it sure seemed that way. There was no need to wonder whether all of that was sinful. It had to be, no two ways about it. Not a sin of word or deed or omission but rather, in this case, of thought, and a mortal one at that. I expected nothing less. Fear of burning in the eternal flames, or, more to the point, of deserving to burn in that fire, made me feel wretched and alive.

My uncle slaughtered lambs almost every evening, so that my grandmother would have plenty to slice and sell the following day at the butcher's she ran. I never missed a single killing, my eyes opened wide in astonishment, nor did I bat an eyelid at the sight of that ritual replayed over and over again in silence beneath a naked bulb and dozens of flies hovering nearby. I was seven years old, then eight, then nine, and so on, summer after summer. My grandfather would tether their four legs firmly together with the string used to make bundles of hay, before sharpening his knife on a corner of the barnyard wall, now worn away, then slit their throats from one side to another, gripping them tight between his other hand and his left knee. In no time, the bucket he had set on the floor would fill to the brim with foamy blood. One of the high points was when, after slicing a lamb open down the middle, he would pluck out its digestive apparatus almost in one piece, removing the small intestine, which was sold separately to make guitar strings, before tossing it over the door to the pigsty, whereupon the pigs began to fight one another amid horrendous squeals to devour those still-throbbing guts that were giving off a small cloud of steam. I have always been wary of connecting all of this to the butchery I dreamt of at church during those endless masses, but there's no denying that I had the first erection I can recall the day on which my uncle allowed me to pick out and seize the lamb to be slaughtered that night from a group of six or eight he had set aside beforehand in a section of the pen that was, for the sheep, a death row of sorts. This was less and less a laughing matter; I was God back then, in every sense of the word. The lambs piled into one corner, clambering on top of one another, each of them looking at me with eyes that have crept into my dreams a thousand times over. Though they would all meet the same deadly fate in a matter of days, the fact remains that that night, I handed down death sentences and pardons and understood in my own way what the catechists were getting at when they spoke of divine glory. And my spirits would soar. Then, I'd feel sad and yet at the same time proud at having been able to shoulder, my head held high, my share of the hangman's burden. And I remember that getting any sleep that night was out of the question—for my thoughts turned constantly to that jet of blood streaming into the bucket, all of that red foam that was like the juice of my guilt—and that I could not for a moment stop thinking of the power and the glory. Wide awake, I leant over the balcony in the early hours of the morning and felt, for the very first time, that all of the stars were on my side.

Some years later, I aimed the semen from one of the first masturbations of my life into the handbag of one of my mother's friends. Visitors to the house would pile coats, scarves, umbrellas, and the like on top of a bed in the room closest to the front door. I went in and did that in the half-darkness, quite why I'm not sure. Perhaps because she was the prettiest and youngest of the female friends who would drop by for afternoon tea from time to time, and the one who best hooked one leg over the other as she sat down in the little side room for coffee and cake, not to mention the only one whose nails were always painted maroon, not only on Sundays, and I wanted those hands of hers, so soft, when fumbling around for something inside her handbag, to be stained with the semen that was the product of a love and a fever that, deep down, was hers by every right. Queen of all she surveyed. That semen was her doing, fruit of her harvest, the consequence of a desire she had worked for beforehand—whether consciously or otherwise, that's neither here nor there—when brushing her hair that afternoon at the dressing table, when picking out her dress and trying it on in front of the mirror, turning this way and that, when covering her skin with lotions. I liked to imagine the look on her face, the grimace of disgust when she discovered her hands soiled with God knows what, so sticky, her sunglasses tainted with me, her small leather-bound address book with the telephone numbers of the men who'd buy her cocktails on Saturdays, her lipstick, and all those little bottles of eau de cologne, and the lacquer for those nails that never clawed my back.

I think of love now and I always picture the same dark room, much like the one in which the coats were

159

left, the blinds partly muffling the noise of the street, the unbearable light of day, and a gray sheet damp with sweat, on which to lie while everything settles back down, barely saying a word, next to a body that just moments ago was nothing but moans and cries and frenzied desire and that now lies vanquished, still trembling a little, ravishing and filthy in the half-light. A summer afternoon in the city and wondering what is to become of us, how to fight against the flesh that binds us and drains us and satiates us and tosses us through the air, how we can go on living from now on without eating one another alive, without hurting each other, without having to crawl after the other's desire each time one of us leaves and the other returns and the yearning draws blood and only flies come to the wound. Down what slope we shall tumble when the city comes to a standstill in the middle of a barren summer and we no longer have each other or anything other than the memory of all this like a torment, the imprint of my fingers on your buttocks while Miles Davis played and the candle flame flickered out atop a pink mound of melted wax. Sometimes, the punishment for the pain that is to come already lies, like a down payment, in the fury of love, when it brandishes its claws and is unleashed for real from the deepest depths of the blood, and when caresses and lashes of the whip, honeyed kisses and brutal thrusts all blend into one. Vengeance for the tears that have not yet but will no doubt be shed, sooner rather than later, and for the solitude that lies ahead and the sorrow of the evenings and yet more evenings, on the other side of a season or two, when memories will linger of the vertigo of this soft skin slammed against the wall, the hiss of the riding crop through the air, the parted lips that in the semi-darkness plead for punishment and mercy at one and the same time. Perhaps love is not the word, then. Perhaps it is not the word at all if the hips we hold firmly in our grasp, sinking our nails into them, are always those of a cheap whore and all of the pain that lies in wait, even when it has yet to take shape or come into being, is already seeping out from somewhere and drips onto our back in the darkness.

Today I remember, in no particular order, some of the women who passed through that bedroom that was not always the same one, much though it might be in my memory, as if the bed were a flying ship that traveled through time in every direction while also moving from city to city. Some of them I all but wrestled into bed. For the most part, though, their hips swaying a couple of steps ahead of me, they willingly climbed the staircase, with its plant pots and its cats, up to that bedroom, its window muffling the ever-present noise of the traffic in different streets in different cities and the ambulance sirens wailing down there below, on the asphalt, heading to the La Paz, the 12 de Octubre, and the Casa Grande hospitals.

While most of the women I chose, insofar as they were mine to choose, had their dark side, there were others whom I snatched straight from the light, above all in the early days. I plucked them from gentle worlds in which they were happy in their own way, flitting cheerfully between their English lessons and their piano lessons, their Wednesdays at the swimming pool, their Friday tango classes with an Argentine instructor, their afternoons at the library highlighting veritable mountains of photocopied notes with felt-tip pens of every color, with their adorable short-sightedness, with their hair tied up so as to be able to let it down if and when the mood took them, when the time came, with the simple gesture of removing their hair band and placing it on their wrist, by way of a bracelet, to make sure it didn't vanish as if by magic on a bedside table overflowing with stuff (earrings, a box of tissues, used condom wrappers, tea lights, a small pile of books, a lamp, an ashtray), then putting it back on before heading home by ten to set the table in great haste for a dinner at which they often went without dessert as punishment for having lost their temper when arguing with their fathers about the class struggle, about Cuba as a beacon of hope for the people, or about the Cold War. That was one sort; and then there were others, yet more radiant, who came later, as if in batches, touched by the rays of the Sun God, with flowers in their hair and white bicycles that slept in the living rooms of their apartments, leaning against the wall, just another animal among the many that stretched their limbs amid the cushions that always lay strewn on the floor. There were several of their type, and I've never understood why. Those girls never ate dinner at ten at their parents' place. Indeed, they never had dinner anywhere. They'd grab a yogurt and a piece of fruit. If ever a girl used the word *piece* when discussing fruit without being on a diet, it was because she was mixed up in some weird meditation and balance vibe; those were the worst, they liked to carry little bottles of water around in their pockets and would not be separated from them. I know their sort well—they end up hating you because you smoke and also because they know that, much as they might desire you, they will never be able to love you. They hate you because they figure you won't brush your teeth as often as you should. They hate you because it's plain to see that it'll never work. I don't know why, but my life has always been well-stocked, rather too generously for my liking, with women of that ilk, considering how much trouble they've always given me, for the fact is I've never been able to peel a simple tomato, chop an onion, or dress a salad worthy of the name. Come to that, I still hate salad, even more so one that's been smothered, as those girls were wont to do, with soy sprouts or brewer's yeast. To this day, the absurd consensus that holds all such things, salad in particular, to be edible still strikes me as utterly conventional, arbitrary, and hare-brained. I don't like riding a bike, either, nor do I understand the need to spend the whole day discussing herbal teas and types of honey. There are, by all accounts, many types of honey. Lavender honey, so they told me, albaida honey, thyme honey, rosemary honey, orange blossom honey. Though, as far as I'm concerned, it's hard to tell one apart from another and they all share the same common denominator of being sticky and foul. And yet I have never strayed too far from that world of bikes secured to the staircase railings in the patio or at the door to indie bars, next to the notice board announcing yoga, street theater, and tantric sex courses, that world of sticks of incense burning nonstop and all that crappy whole grain and raw sugar. Which begs the question: What was I doing there if I hated, with every ounce of my being, all that inner balance bullshit, the kettledrums, the baggy pants, the dancing on the sand, and if it was clear to me that my life's best moments have always taken place with a brimming ashtray and a clutter of glasses and empty bottles nearby, adding, for the truly memorable ones, clothes strewn on the floor, torn, if possible, and a record that goes on spinning well into the night with the first light of dawn, the world now broken, shoulders slumped, defenses in disarray thanks to all that poison guzzled without a second thought? Perhaps the answer is that, contrary to popular belief, the opposite of love is not hate—the opposite of love is revulsion. For I was searching for something in those women who lay barefoot on the campus lawns in their long skirts, like Indian princesses, and who, in my darkest hours, took me into their clouds of incense and marihuana smoke and soothed my nerves, taking me for walks through the gardens separating the different department buildings from the parking lots, pointing out the trees and their names, this leaf, that branch. Something like ensnaring moments of peace in my nets, moments of a light I never knew how to use and all I could do was devour it later on, at the hour when the moon takes its leave and the wolves remain, at the back of a lair, when the night is dirty and pure darkness sweating and spinning. Those girls wanted to take to the air with me, and that was love, the clean air of a certain paradise they seemed to know beforehand, while I needed to be led astray, to ask questions, to grope around for the path, to stumble and to bleed, to fall from the cliff tops holding tight to their hips.

I can only think back on the true loves of my life in the dark, and only when I am alone and feel I have the strength. I can still be left shaken by the sound of a handful of women's names. For the time being, I have no wish to name them, so as not to hear the sound my heart makes down there when, instead of ageing at its normal rate, it races headlong toward death. I know I do so in my dreams—say their names, that is—for I have sometimes woken myself up calling out to them. One of them sleeps naked in my head, a lifeless arm hanging limply in the air like Jacques-Louis David's *Marat*; another, the one who would squat down to take snapshots of all of the cats in the neighborhood of Lavapies peeking out from the patios or sleeping on sawdust in bars, is sobbing, though neither of us will ever know why; and I can see another girl returning from the bookshop in Cuatro Caminos holding a copy of the *Diary of Anaïs Nin* and a recently shoplifted anthology by Alejandra Pizarnik. The rain is beating down in the street, and she has buried the books deep inside her handbag so as not to ruin them. I remember the scent of the raindrops in her hair and the inscription she wrote me in one of those books: "May your sadness shatter into a thousand pieces in the air like the dandelion on which a small boy has blown with all his might, like a swan shot down in mid-flight, like a Civil Guard." Her room is filled with photos of female writers who took their own lives, tacked onto the wall with pushpins, and self-penned sketches showing Sylvia Plath with her head in the oven, Virginia Woolf flailing in the middle of the current, and Alfonsina Storni advancing, vacant and zombie-like, toward the center of an ocean filled with black waves rearing up. She would like to have been Max Ernst's lover, but she stayed by my side, sometimes curled up in a ball at my feet and sometimes pulling on me in her flight to the center of the storms. She was anyone's match drinking gin, and when she was tipsy she could sing Janis Joplin's

"Mercedes Benz" all the way through, falling into a lengthy silence when she was done, somewhere between exhaustion and oblivion. I always remember her with her bangs plastered against her sweaty brow. The neighbors were no fans of her early morning singing or the noise she made when she bumped into the furniture when she got up to vomit, not to mention her outrageous orgasms, making many a night a veritable war of pounding back and forth on the walls, with fists, with the sole of a shoe, to see who might give in first, until everything settled down more or less at the hour when the subway opened and the streets, still in darkness, began filling up with sleepwalkers making their way to offices and factories.

Life back then was on a knife's edge between hell and warmth, anguished silence and cries of joy. Somehow we knew, no matter how fiercely tedium struck, that a well-chosen song or a bottle of something or other would always end up coming to our rescue. It was a matter of bearing witness to our own collapse without losing heart altogether, the paradox of having to kill ourselves in order to carry on living, like insects that feed off limbs ripped from their own bodies with their own teeth. Our wound was the show, and its condition, the highlight of the day, a sort of regular report giving an account of the state of the rot that had set in there in the gut, like a gangrene advancing like hordes on horseback, the liver swelling millimeter by millimeter as it turns to cardboard, the ever-stranger dreams in which the lizard in the sake bottle sometimes danced with the worms in the mescal bottle, the candles at the mercy of the night's winds, infinity all set to be conquered, the valium, the tears, the transaminases.

I see myself lying on the bed in the morning, forcing myself to smoke a cigarette without succumbing to a coughing fit that will, in turn, make my stomach churn even more. A girl is sleeping with her head on my chest, her hair is dirty, it smells of smoke, that hair, and of cold ash. There is a nausea inside my chest that gives occasional signs of life. My nerves dance around that nausea like stripped wires, like anemone writhing around on raw flesh. The minute hand barely advances, as if hauling a great weight behind it, the world is a slow-motion blur, out of focus, upside down at times; though I cannot see it from my bed, I picture a blue earth and trees hanging from a sky filled all of a sudden with puddles. I try to think back to what happened the night before but soon realize that I can't bear to find out. When memory returns, it does so like a monster emerging from the mist and skewering my shame with the tip of its spear. The mind starts rowing full tilt in the opposite direction, toward the void, trying to blend in with the nothingness, to empty itself of thoughts as far as possible, conjuring up snowy expanses free, if possible, of horizons or footprints, and boreal skies, and calm oceans. To not think, to remember nothing, to make sure the floodgates hold firm, to do whatever it takes rather than come to terms with the unbearable, the images from the night before that begin to stir and take shape, making their presence felt against my wishes. Like a dog defending a farmyard to the death, my nausea growls at the memories that little by little dare to show their faces. It imagines machine guns opening fire at random in every direction. It unleashes a round in my face at point-blank range, it dreams of wiping me off the face of the earth and from history, it fantasizes about snatching me from the minds of others. The water's surface in the green plastic jug that lives on my bedside table is covered with dust and the odd hair of a cat or God knows who. I drink from that water. All of a sudden I find it fresh and appetizing, and for a moment it tastes of the life I lost, as leafy as the paths I walked straight past or left behind me, one that followed the course of the river, for example, leading to an abandoned windmill at the bottom of the Añisclo canyon, near a small meadow in which I would sit to wolf down spoonfuls of all the honey I spurned and even the very flowers I laughed at, now that the refrigerator is empty but for the smell of wine now drunk and these dry parsley leaves stuck to the plastic walls.

Sometimes, as the month neared its end, we'd steal food from the cat, spreading its Whiskas on slices of bread. But whenever we had a little money to spend, the neighborhood of Malasaña was ours for the taking. We'd always start out in Corripio, right across from the drugstore on the Calle Fuencarral, with Asturian chorizo pie and draft cider to help a few shots of neat absinthe slip down all the easier, before moving on to bottled beer in El Maragato, where we delighted in the foul tempers of the old couple who ran the place and who we knew would end up serving us Roquefort sandwiches on the house. Later, despite my protests (all my attempts to convince her to leave it be were to no avail), she'd insist on heading off in search of Leopoldo María Panero, with whom she had struck up something of a friendship one strange night on which it was I who ended up sleeping with him and one Alicia, the one who collected the corpse, according to the dedication in *Narciso*, and who stayed up till dawn, licking the poet's toes the whole night through. If Leopoldo had been let out of the madhouse, he'd turn up sooner or later on one street or another. With his cohort of groupies and aspiring court jesters in tow, hoping some of his doomed-poet aura might rub off on them. He was always wandering around as if hoping to get his ass kicked, and on more than one occasion he got his wish in the end. I remember the floor in El Valle, covered in sawdust, mussel shells, and olive pits, and Leopoldo writhing around on that floor in his raincoat, unleashing an awful cackle straight out of a horror movie. He liked to urinate in the middle of the street, in every direction, spinning around, standing square in the center of the night beneath a witch's moon, its dark side and visible side drenched in a beery sweat. His madness was legendary and beautiful. I remember his black corduroy pants, too, his long raincoat, his feet on the table, any table, occasionally knocking the glasses of rum and Coke to the floor while reciting unintelligible verses that spoke of ruins, of fly-eaten brains, and of the disaster that is living. He'd get in people's faces on the slightest pretext, brandishing his fists at the drop of a hat and aping the poses boxers like to strike in the photos taken for the posters, accusing any waiter who dared take him to task for his behavior or throw him straight out of the bar of being a fascist, unaware as they were that he was the star of the disenchantment, the prince of the madcap night, the light shimmering at the bottom of all our wells.

I look back on that time as a tug-of-war between despair and ecstasy. It was at one and the same time yearning and regret, a banquet of intensity with its towers and its ruins, vomit and joy. Writing on napkins in bars, returning home with bloodied eyebrows, with my shirt in tatters, without knowing how or at what point it had happened. It was the almost daily police raids in and around the square, the vans filled with laughing, toothless whores, the early mornings at the precinct on the Calle Madera, and also the rush of knowing oneself to be alive while never ceasing to row in the opposite direction. I believe I once got laid in the very doorway on the Calle Espíritu Santo in which Enrique Urquijo's dead body was found, I'd venture that I wrote the most beautiful and horrifying verses the world has ever known on scraps of paper I later lost, and I'd even swear that I was myself somehow beautiful, seated in the doorways of bars, missing the last subway home after lingering to listen to some street musicians before returning home on foot, my pockets empty, dizzy beneath the sky of two or three different neighborhoods, only to find a cat starving to death and a lukewarm bed that had a direct line to gaps in the memory down which I could fall.

And I cannot separate my idea of love from all that, from that lost state, and I identify it with the last-ditch, futile attempt of a fear to ally itself with another fear, as if the two could be one, and with permeable souls in place of that fortified citadel that cannot be breached no matter what side you're on. Which is why love always has that air of chasing the impossible and is, by nature, tragic, or barely even exists. I can only conceive of it as a sort of shared bewilderment, two souls looking in the same direction, barely able to see a thing, without knowing where to turn, and transforming the world, behind the cobwebs that filter the gaze, into a labyrinth. It calls for two lost beings, two deviants who brush up against each other in the dark, then drift apart, before running into one another again. The interlocking hands must tremble in some way. Which explains Marta. Which explains the faltering steps that came later, the cocaine without restraint, the black seas, the ship in flames, and the wails in the night, the caresses that amounted to little more than our trembling hands, the bad trips, the messages of hate written in lipstick on the mirror, the broken glasses, the torn panties, the tracks left by fingernails on our backs, before, in the end, falling asleep in each other's embrace like newborn puppies from the same litter, exhausted and skinny, scared stiff.

Which begs the question: Why did a handful of photos and a voice on the other end of the line bring back a world now long gone? Perhaps it helps that I got my hands on the photos under cover of night, vaulting over the barriers, looking where I ought not to look, in the spirit of a spy betraying his fatherland unbeknownst even to his own family, or a mother trying not to make a sound as she masturbates in front of the computer screen while the children are sleeping. And perhaps the fact that Nadia called me in secret also has a part to play, that all but inaudible whisper that gave away her fear of being caught holding the phone, and the knowledge that I was speaking to an adulteress, and the word *adulteress*. Which begs the question: What role did her appearance on the scene also have to play in relation to a brutal crime, to an axe concealed behind a door, and a blood stain on the wall you cannot get out no matter how hard you scrub? And it begs the question, above all, of why the battle-scarred never learn, why they keep coming back for more after all that fighting.

If the business of living is above all a matter of betraying, one by one, the dreams that fuelled our childhood and younger years, then each person is the exact sum total of a good number of betrayals. Hundreds in some cases. The purest of dreams are betrayed, as are nightmares. By mistake, we flee from storms without ever realizing that they were such a part of who we are and were so ingrained in our very cores that without them we barely amount to a thing. Save me, we say, I no longer wish to plunge a knife into your legs, we say, I will not hurt you, I will not want to see your grimace of pain in the mirror, I will love you in another way, I will worship you from a being that does not exist, I will call my past a torment, an agony until I met you. I will tell you that you are as gentle as the sky I dream and that I do not mind closing my eyes to everything forevermore if I know that you will later kiss my eyelids. I will not be me. I will bury the monster beneath spadefuls and yet more spadefuls of earth. I will get as close to nothingness as it is possible to get, to a coffin without a dead man, to an empty cathedral. I will buy you flowers.

It cannot be all that hard, for nothing is what we are in essence, when the time comes to tear off the disguise—the list jotted down in a notebook of things left undone, the slew of countless arrows that never left the bow, together with those that were lost, somewhere further than the eye can see. A large bunch of beautiful betrayals, as big as suns. And that bunch and nothing more is all we ought to offer each other when making promises of love, if indeed love is the word. Everything else is untrue. That meager bouquet, and nothing more—look, Nadia, this faded poppy losing its color as fast as fear can strike is in fact, you might say, a life I never lived on the far side of the Atlantic, whether in the mining regions of Chile or the outskirts of Zipaquirá, in that bar with the corrugated roof that stood beside the highway; this intact daisy is a woman, one among many, barefoot beneath the pouring rain, from whom I once turned away and to whom I said nothing, though I could have when her eyes may well have been pointing me in the direction of a doorway in the Latin Quarter, a *chambre de bonne*, a pair of panty hose to be ripped apart once and for all before tossing them into the trash, a huge dry white towel with room enough for the both of us; this iris trembling in my fingers stands for a couple of languages I never learned, though I thought I might, and the infinite silence made up of all of the words I left unsaid in those languages; and this rose with entranced petals is the sum of the alleyways whose shadows cried out to me and down which, when push came to shove, I did not dare to venture. Look, in short, at these half-broken flowers, we should tell one another, instead of all that cringe-worthy baloney we spout in such circumstances, look at these flowers that come apart at the touch of a finger like a butterfly's wings, together they go to make up who I am. The two of us are made of the things we never did, we are the rage and the foam of the countless renunciations that interlock with one another like links on a chain, the foul temper that remained after watching as things and trains passed us by, and the calm that came in its wake, the hours, the drowsiness, the grit beneath the eyelids upon waking. We are that dirty nothingness. And if we have learned anything from all that resentment, all that coming and going, all that sorrow of mistimed steps and almost always empty hands, we should, at most, offer each other something that amounts to little more than this: let us renounce together, let us share a dream of something we will never do, whatever it is, a house with a garden, a round-the-world trip, let us join together both nothing-nesses, let us intertwine these two lives that were left behind unlived, the barely glimpsed stories of two creatures who held back when the time came to run and who beat a hasty retreat when they should have stayed put, let us daydream of landscape that will never envelop us, the ships, the cities, the forests seen from trains, the image of our feet dangling from atop a skyscraper overlooking Central Park or an Irish cliff top beneath which furious green waves roar. But no more promises spoken in earnest, the heart exposed, for promises in earnest are a lie, no more desire of the sort that turns to poison when it comes into contact with the skin. Never again, my love, never again this exhausting pursuit of delirium, of two becoming one, and that one standing happily in the center of the wind.

17

(intimacy)

Nadia arrived at our meeting ten minutes late. I don't know why, but I'd assumed she'd turn up much later. I positioned myself in the bar next to one of the windows, so as to be able to see her as she appeared around the street corner. As I watched her approach, I wondered what it might be like to miss her. In other words, what it might be like to have loved her dearly, for a long time, only for her then to have left.

In the flesh, she looked slightly plumper than in her photos. Pretty, either way, with extremely close-cropped blonde hair, à la Jean Seberg, and very dark skin. It wasn't until after talking to her for a few minutes, with her observing you from very close quarters, that you could truly appreciate her allure. She had that trait, such a hard one to come by, that can make a man lose his head and drive him to perdition in record time. By which I mean a sort of contrast, a contradiction even, between the eyes and the mouth. While the gaze is a gentle combination of innocence and melancholy, the lips, just a few inches further down, slightly parted, summon forth the wildest of desires. Not everyone can see it. I have rarely come across such a clear-cut case. Marilyn Monroe, perhaps, in certain photos. Not in every one, that's for sure. But there are some in which, if you cover the entire image with your hands aside from the eyes, you are left with the gaze of someone pleading for protection and tenderness, perhaps even consolation. And if you then do the same, but this time leaving only the mouth in view, what you get is a fragment of a photograph with which any teenager could happily lock himself away in the bathroom to go about his business. When she spoke, depending on which phoneme she was uttering, you could see the tip of Nadia's tongue. Without realizing it, she promised everything when she spoke.

I filled her in on how the past few days had been for me—the extent of Jacobo's terror the last night I went to keep him company, his fear, for the first time, not of the waves of anguish to which he had more or less become accustomed, insofar as anyone can get used to such a thing, but rather of human beings to be fended off with knives and blunt objects. I explained how unhinged the whole business had left me, how, out of instinct, I had begun by searching his apartment and had ended up combing my own place, which I had been unable ever since to see as anything other than a dead man's home. I told her how, in the wake of the murder, I had become a stranger among my own things, that sense of having outlived myself, transformed into a shadow, and how I had assumed the role of a nosy relative who prizes open drawers and breaks padlocks, who fingers sacred objects and ends up reading letters that were not meant for his eyes, looking at photos of himself as if they were showing him the face of a stranger, keenly studying the passages underlined in books, sorting through bills, train tickets, coasters, receipts of every kind, and programs for theaters that have long since ceased to exist.

She told me she hadn't been in Zaragoza for long. She said she'd gotten separated a couple of years back and had ever since been looking to make a clean break. She had, quite literally, had a makeover; she'd even chosen a new name. She also said that she'd been hoping to move but was not sure where to or when, she was still at that stage where you dream of impossible houses hugging the sea, with a porch and plants creeping up freshly whitewashed walls. She added that she wasn't cut out for the single life. As for Jacobo, it was clear that she preferred not to go into too much detail. Truth be told, she didn't wish to go into too much detail about anything. It was as if she were striving to make everything she said sound banal. The first time they met, Jacobo had insisted that she read *The War* by Marguerite Duras. They had arranged to meet so that he could lend her his copy then made another date to discuss the book. It puzzled Nadia how anyone could become so obsessed over a story that, as she saw it, was like so many others. "Like so many others," that's how she put it. They became lovers. It's not as if they saw much of one another. Nor did they have a shared future mapped out or plans of any kind. They simply called each other from time to time whenever either of them felt loneliness beginning to bite, a feeling, as anyone will tell you, that tends to wax and wane. They cooked meals for each other, sampled new wines, and then went to bed, usually somewhat tipsy. At this point,

Nadia's gestures take on a coy air that I do not fully buy. There are no observations, no details. She averts her gaze, seeking refuge in a short pause in order to take another sip of her coffee, only her cup is already empty.

All of a sudden, she tells me she'd like to go to Jacobo's apartment. She asks if I've got the keys on me.

"Well, no, I don't have the keys on me."

"I do. Here, in my bag."

"Right, then you can go any time."

"Not alone."

"Perhaps you've already been."

"No. I can't bring myself to go alone, I told you. I'd like you to come with me now. It'll only take a couple of minutes."

"Are you sure? You might find it painful."

"I need that pain. I feel like ice, right now, and I can't stand it. I just want to be there for a moment, to take a quick look around, to remember the smells. Then tonight, when I go to bed, I'll try to break down in tears. That's the idea."

Once inside the apartment, she began to make her way very slowly from room to room, peering out the window several times. She barely paused in the part of the entryway where the events had taken place, nor did she glance for more than a second or two at the stains of blood encrusted on the stippled wall. Then she lit a cigarette and sat down on one end of the couch. I guess that must have been her spot when they settled in to watch a movie or chat for a while. She wanted a drink. I fixed her a whisky with a couple of ice cubes that smelled a little, it seemed to me, of the hake fillets that had lain next to them in the freezer. Glass in hand, she got up again and headed, very slowly, for the bedroom. There was something robotic in her movements, her gaze did not settle on anything in particular, and yet at the same time it was as if she were scanning everything, before processing it all in the most neutral fashion. She came to a halt, standing before the bed that was now home only to one of the those standard-issue blue mattresses, without a bedspread, that bore, in the form of stains and patches, the traces of all of the apartment's former tenants over time, circles of saliva, sweat, semen, piss, and blood, all the warmth of human intimacy. There, looking at that deformed, empty mattress, she began to cry softly. The statue came to life in its white dress. "Son of a bitch," she said. I went to fetch a wad of toilet paper and handed it to her by way of a handkerchief. Then, finger by finger, I prized the glass from her grip to prevent it from shattering under the pressure, before placing it on the bedside table. I was just about to say something about how dreadful the moment was and how beautiful she looked, crying at the foot of that bed, wearing the very sandals she was buckling in the photo, without knowing where to tap the ash from the cigarette she held between her fingers or what to do with that sudden stab of pain or where to direct all the desire that sprang from her, perverse and unwelcome, as she looked at that furniture and that light. I was just about to ruin it all with words, but I held back. I simply walked over to where she stood and embraced her from behind, almost recklessly. I could tell that she was thankful, so I hugged her to me. She titled her head back, feeling for me. She also thrust her ass out, feeling for me yet more and without altogether stopping from crying. Snatches of a tango sung by good old Roberto Goyeneche—*qué me importa perderme mil veces la vida*—drifted through the inner patio from some distant radio. And we fell onto the unmade bed just as the first rumblings of a storm that threatened to take with it in a matter of seconds the little evening light that remained could be heard on the other side of the window, and everything was strange and bitter and stunningly beautiful, the white dress on the dried-out filth, my tongue amongst her tears, the pleasure, the anguish, the sobs. Afterward, we lay there a good long while, naked and in silence, very still, watching as the darkness took possession of the dead man's room and listening to the sounds that drifted up from the street, the drip-drip of drainpipes and cornices, the motorcycles driving past, the noise of tires on wet asphalt. And then I think Nadia hit the right note. I will never know how she knew, or what dark magic moved her tongue, but she rested her head on my shoulder, and I'd swear she said *what is to become of us?* And I knew then that I would die calling out her name, and also that she would not come.

After showering, I dried myself off with a used towel of Jacobo's that hung forgotten behind the bathroom door and which seemed to me to smell of a mixture of damp and of him. More specifically, of leaks sprung in the walls of patios and of a grinning Jacobo appearing in that patio, sweating a little, his fishing rod over one shoulder.

18

(squeaking bedsprings)

Marguerite Duras began an affair with Dionys Mascolo, with whom she had joined the Resistance. Meanwhile, her husband, and comrade to the two of them in that freedom-fighting movement, had been taken prisoner in the Dachau extermination camp. They had given him up for dead, more or less. When the camps were liberated, they searched for him high and low, they combed every office, they made phone calls to all and sundry, they despaired at the rumors, they listened to the tales told by the first survivors then reaching Paris in dribs and drabs. Antelme and Mascolo were good friends. The three of them were good friends, in fact. The love between Marguerite and Mascolo blossomed against the backdrop of an absence that neither could bear, which managed to turn their desire for each other into the worst of betrayals and an anguished uncertainty that would make them picture their friend almost always at death's door, a mass of wounds lying on the ground, the final, weary beats of a heart against the mud of some road or other, a fever that shivers alone, its whereabouts unknown, or a shadow coming apart at the seams atop a cot on which the blood soaks through the mattress. The bond that united the new lovers was made from the same barbed wire that had crossed the continent from south to north along the entire length of the Maginot Line, that pointless scar measuring mile after endless mile.

One day the telephone rang, bringing them the news that Antelme was alive. Still alive, miraculously— weighing in at just under seventy pounds in a far-flung infirmary. Mascolo did not think twice. He managed to get his hands on a beat-up old vehicle and went off in search of his friend across a Europe that was little more than a vast expanse of ruins and ashes and cripples and prisoners filing past in every direction, columns of trucks, ghostly convoys on the gravel roads; everywhere you looked there were orphans lining up to beg for soup, flags trampled underfoot, border crossings, their turrets now fallen, newly abandoned casemates, trenches of mist. He brought his friend back as best he could in the back seat of the car, shivering beneath a heap of blankets. Antelme was a bag of bones, eaten away by typhus, who had to be fed spoonfuls of water nonstop and who would break down in sobs without knowing where he was or scarcely even who he was with. They put him to bed, they looked after him for days on end, the two of them, Marguerite and Mascolo, for they both loved him. For he was their friend. They whiled away the hours with him, they spoon-fed him his medicines, they took pains to listen to all of the disjointed horror of his memories, the scream of his ever-present nightmare, the words now devoid of any feeling that might contain a glimmer of hope. They did this for him, for what he had meant and continued to mean to them, in what went to make up their innermost selves. But also, darkly, to make amends for a love too redolent of a stab in the back. In *The War*, Duras writes, "He stopped asking questions about what had happened while he was away. He stopped seeing us. A great, silent pain spread over his face because he was still being refused food, because it was still as it had been in the concentration camp. And, as in the camp, he accepted it in silence. He didn't see that we were weeping. Nor did he see that we could scarcely look at him or respond to what he said."

Antelme could no doubt hear them fucking in the room next door. A lot of fucking goes on in wartime, when you've seen so many comrades fallen in the dirt and death assails you from all sides; a time of fear is also a time of love. Perhaps, at least at first, his mind was unable to pinpoint the exact meaning of that panting that reached him through the partition wall, the rhythmic squeaking of the bedsprings in the early morning hours. Those sounds probably mingled in his delirium with some sort of torture he had lived through or imagined weeks previously— snapped limbs, torn flesh. As he gathers his strength little by little and his eyes once again open to the world and he starts to grasp, as best he can, a little of what is going on around him, he will continue to hear them fucking behind the partition wall of his bedroom and will be unable to move, there will be nowhere to hide from that horror. But then the sun will come up and the two of them will come in together to wish him a good morning, they will feed him the vitamins and tonics procured for a king's ransom on the black market, they will shave him, wash his hair, spoon-feed him soup, with all the patience in the world, as well as his syrup and painkillers—he has no right to protest, much less can he hate them, for even hatred calls for a degree of strength. Marguerite loves him with all her heart, but love is not enough. It hardly ever is. Sometimes all that love, that immense feeling, is no match for a miserable fuck. Another person's desire, with all of its ebb and flow, is the most precise expression of hell.

I have been Robert Antelme on many a night. I have felt his nightmare dampen my brow. The wall is not always a wall. It might be the other side of the street, or several neighborhoods of a city, but that won't silence the bedsprings. The weaker the heart, the better it imitates that sound and the more moans and words it adds in for good measure. I have also on the odd occasion assumed the role of Dionys Mascolo, throwing myself into the task without a care for my surroundings or for what might lie on the other side of a partition wall. Once, my teenage years not far behind me, I screwed the girl my brother had set his heart on, while he lay sleeping in the room next door. I remember tiptoeing into his room in the middle of the night to see if I might find more condoms on his bedside table or in the pockets of his pants, only to find him awake, his eyes moist, and he looked at me as if to say *it's not your fault*, and ever since, pain has always reminded me of that look, in near darkness, offering me forgiveness. When the heart is broken, all the love spills out.

19

(gallows)

Those days with Nadia were the best thing that had happened to me in an awful long time. There were even evenings on which she busied herself knitting while I lay on her sofa, reading peacefully, my feet resting on the cushion she had placed on the coffee table and the two of us covered by the same blanket, which we grew to see as a metaphor for tedium of the sweetest sort. We had for the most part succumbed to a state of gentle melancholy, broken only by the intermittent stabs of savage desire to which we fell prey in the most unlikely moments. We were forever looking at each other, we spoke little, and the silence that enveloped us stood in stark contrast to the frenzied fits of passion that came hot on its heels, the buttons torn off in haste, her tennis player's moans, pinned against the kitchen counter. We ourselves were frightened by that contrast and by our own inability to do anything by halves. Later, barely saying a word, we'd console each other for all the guilt writhing beneath the surface. We asked for each other's forgiveness and never withheld it. She was the mistress of my sorrow, and all of the storms, all of the waves of fear ended up breaking between her legs.

We resolved to head outdoors to see how what we had between us might fare in the open air. The idea was to walk among people, to position ourselves among the rest of the world's things to see how it went, and that aroma, so otherworldly, of pleasure and nightmare, slipped from our skin. We went to see a film at the Eliseo movie theater. Staring straight ahead at the screen, she started fondling me, before resting her head on my shoulder—I could tell she was crying—and, finally, falling asleep. One day, a fierce wind blowing, we took a trip to the old town of Belchite and strolled among the ruins, barely exchanging a word. A plane (one from this century, I think) cut across the sky at one point and made us shiver. Wearing a white headscarf, she sat atop the rubble so that I might photograph her. In those pictures she looks like a frightened Italian refugee amid the ruins of an air raid that's escaped from time. We were forced to beat a hasty retreat when the tower and the walls looked all set to crumble above our heads under the northern wind.

At that time, I returned to the old folks' home to see my mother. In a few short weeks, her memory and general well-being had taken a considerable turn for the worse. She did not ask me to take her to any cemeteries this time. When I made the offer myself, she gave me a puzzled look, as if wondering what on earth she might possibly have to do out there among the graves. I was pleased that she had forgotten about death and, in general, the causes of a sorrow that now lived as if untethered within her, now just a free-floating nebula. The sorrow that could still be seen in her expression seemed purely a matter of force of habit. There comes a point when the composition of a face—the wrinkles, the bags under the eyes, the gaze—serves only to look sad. By then, it is already too late for any redemption. I don't think she had the slightest idea who I was, aside from the fact that my voice and my face may have struck her as vaguely familiar.

"Listen up a minute, please, tell me something: Do you know who I am?"

She tried to dodge the question, but I repeated it. And without taking my eyes off hers, up close, I forced her to reply.

"Well, no, I don't know," she said at last, "the truth is I don't know. But something very close to my heart."

Then she began telling me, one more time, the story of her friend Gisia Paradís. I knew that the story, in her mouth, was not a long one, so I made no protest, and I summoned all my patience and sat back to listen again, as if it were the very first time, to the old, familiar exploits of my mother's friend. How pretty she was, how much they had loved each other as young girls, and how her friend had left the lovely Provincia with hopes of becoming an actress—that's how gorgeous she was—and of making it big in the capital and all that jazz. Though she ended up plying her trade in a few movies between '59 and '67, all the talk back in her hometown, always in somewhat hushed tones, was of poor Gisia, her head in the clouds, her flings with men and maybe, who knows, with drugs. Taken for a ride, abused. They all liked to picture the girl, her mascara smeared by tears, in one of those dens of iniquity that stay open all night long, lit up in red, a glass

in her hand and all her dreams lying on the floor. And
my mother told me how one day, in some local festival,
her friend had turned up in the lovely Provincia on board
a white Mercedes, bigger and shinier than the sort they
rented out for a fortune when the great and the good
tied the knot back in those days, and how she descended
from the car in much the same way the great artists of
the day alighted from theirs, feigning a clumsiness that
would allow them to drag the process out a second or two
more, knees on display for all to see and skirt hiked up
an inch or too higher than might be deemed reasonable,
just as the flashes of the throng of photographers waiting
at the door to the theatre went off, almost in unison. And
she told me how Gisia's door was opened by a gentleman
who one second before, in the manner of a presidential
bodyguard, had dashed around from the other side of
the car, and that gentleman was none other than Carlos
Larrañaga. Carlos Larrañaga, no less. And how that instant
was worth an entire lifetime, for even though Gisia was to
meet a premature end not long after, the event had been
witnessed by the whole town, and she had managed—
without entirely wanting to, mind, for she wasn't like that,
Gisia was always such a sweetheart, what light she gave
off—to rub all their noses in it, triumphantly watching,
albeit for that one day only, as their envy was all of a
sudden struck dumb, the glances of astonishment, the
silenced blabbermouths, the speed at which the smugness
of those fine folks gave way to rage and bafflement among
that cluster of ladies, some with their husbands hanging
from their arms, all pressed up against the security fences
and even dressed up in all their finery, fresh from the

neighborhood hairdresser's, who looked like parrots, if not down-and-outs, at Gisia's side. Ever since I was a child, I have always wondered why my mother was so drawn to that simple story and above all why, against her nature, she flew in the face of all of her neighbors and championed the dazzling downfall of Gisia Paradís, standing up for a life she imagined to be filled with everything she found most reprehensible: late-night bars, drugs she couldn't even name, mornings in strange beds, bags of ice for aching heads, gifts from gentlemen to be pawned off for a pitiful sum to cover the rent. No doubt the key to her loyalty lay in the fact that as young girls, back in their neighborhood days, lying on the ground and gazing up at the summer sky, the pair of them had spoken of their dreams and of everything they hoped to make of their lives, and had wished each other luck with a sincerity that perhaps no longer exists in adult life. I also think that what my mother truly envied about her friend was not her wayward artistic ways in search of life in the city at night, or her dresses, or the fact that she broke out a fresh pair of panty hose every three or four days, or anything else in her world of red lights and slimy producers. What she truly envied was everything her friend had escaped by leaving, the webs she had slipped through, even at the cost of ruining her own life: a wedding in the Church of Santo Domingo, a Seat 600 crammed full of kids heading for La Peña reservoir, ten o'clock mass, the street market on Tuesdays, the chorus lines of windbags waiting for their children at the school gates, eleven o'clock mass, the *Educación y Descanso* union membership card that entitled you to use the swimming pool at a discount, the endless scrubbing, the *Lagarto*-brand bars of soap, the widow's pension, twelve o'clock mass, the Sunday afternoons sipping hot chocolate in dimly lit cafés, the friends who tell you to cheer up and join them for a night on the town, the indignity of it all, the bachelors, the bingo, the defeat.

I saw her looking at me, my mother, trying to figure out exactly who I was. It has always seemed to me that it saddens her to look at me, even now that she no longer knew who stood before her. It's as if my identity had been wiped from her memory before her worry for me, and that worry, which had outlived my name in her brain, was now drifting around in there, bereft and aimless.

Listen, Mom, I'm telling you this precisely because I know that you don't understand me or understand who I am, where this guy talking to you now and taking you by the hand has sprung from, and because, when all is said and done, you'll have forgotten before long: I'm happy now, you know? Not because things are looking up. Things never do, that's just the way of things. It's hard to explain, like this, sitting before one of these foul cups of coffee they serve in here, lukewarm and stomach-churning, so grandmotherly, and with you sitting there in front of me, staring back at me. But I feel I owe it to you, for you have always thought that there was not enough light in my eyes, and you suffered because of that, and you've spent your life searching for some sign of happiness in me, no matter how small. There's this woman, you see? You still asked me about that not even a year ago; so here's the thing, I'll spare you the bit about her name and what she does for a living and all those details that don't matter at all now, but if you only knew, if you could only understand what I feel every time my semen spurts out toward the sky of her mouth, how my heart races at that moment, then perhaps the melancholy that lingers on your face every time you look at me would be wiped away. She runs it over the roof of her mouth, it doesn't disgust her in the slightest. She looks at me as she swallows it, then wipes me off very slowly with a damp towel, all without saying a word, before going back to whatever it was she was doing, just like that, to her book, her knitting. Then, very serious, she crosses her legs again on the other end of the couch as she listens, now without looking at me, to my ragged breathing. Thank you for smiling, Mom. Thank you for not understanding a thing and yet looking at me as if you understood. Guess what? I sometimes take a hundred euros out of your savings account. For this and that, for myself. That's right, at this stage of the game. Me, who not long ago dreamed of buying a house in the country for Dad and you. Now he's dead and I don't know where you are, even though you sit here before me, with those eyes that are the same eyes that have always watched me and which, truth be told, look at first glance like something more than what they actually are: the windows of an uninhabited house.

We saw each other almost every day, Nadia and I. Almost always at her apartment, a spotless, one-room hideout where everything was an immaculate white— the walls, the furniture, the sheets. Though she claimed to live there, it did not take me long to realize she wasn't telling the truth. Late one night, after she had convinced me to sleep back at my place, I waited awhile inside my car, just to see how long it would take her to switch off the lights, and I saw her heading out the front door just minutes after I had left, before hopping on board a waiting cab and disappearing up the street. I repeated the same routine on the following nights and discovered that she always left, she never slept the night there. I, meanwhile, had some trouble sleeping, and on the very few occasions on which we ever spent the whole night together, after she had dozed off, I'd get out of bed and begin exploring the barely more than five hundred square feet, not including the bedroom, of her cramped apartment. If I'd spent the afternoon compulsively searching my own place, I'd find it hard to stop myself from opening the drawers in Nadia's apartment, or, I believe, any other place in which I might find myself. There was something robotic and machine-like in those gestures of a wannabee spy. It took some effort to resist, and in the darkness of the night, my efforts were sometimes to no avail. One of the first things that struck me was the total absence in the apartment of the sort of objects that build up with the simple passing of time, objects that seem to have a life of their own, like insects, and that surreptitiously take possession of rooms and furniture. There was no sign, for instance, of the usual drawer containing bunches of keys for who knows what doors, batteries for the radio, random passport-sized photos, a small sewing kit, plugs that serve no purpose any more, nail clippers, the papers and documents that everyone keeps somewhere or other, spare bulbs, and that sort of thing. There was none of that. Nothing that might make one think of that apartment as somewhere truly lived in. It struck me instead as one of those places that are rented out fully furnished and with all the trimmings, tableware, towels, and kitchen rags included.

During my first search, I found a bunch of red flowers, now dried, inside the trash can, cellophane wrapping and all. Days later, the gold-rimmed card that had no doubt accompanied those flowers turned up, one corner peeking out from beneath the television stand: "My darling Mantis: fresh blood, my own love." It was signed with the initial *I*, and the date coincided exactly with the day on which Jacobo's dead body had been found.

From then on, it was all cars on my tail, long-range telescopes watching over my apartment from hundreds of windows. I went to Jacobo's apartment to fetch his axe and baseball bat and hid them within easy reach, right next to the front door. I tried to stay awake, the lights turned off, I brewed pots of coffee in the near dark and spent my time scrutinizing everything, the noises behind the partition walls, the sliver of light beneath the door. One evening, it seemed to me that the scaffolding of gallows earmarked for me was being built in the next-door apartment. I could hear the sound of a hammer on nails, of timber being hoisted.

I wanted to call on a friend to keep me company, but he was dead. Aside from Nadia, I couldn't think who to turn to. When I called her, she told me I was freaking out, that I was losing my mind for real, and that the best thing I could do was take a strong sedative and go to bed. Everything would look different in the morning light, I'd see. I had to sob down the line to convince her to catch a cab and turn up at my door to help me get through what seemed a terrible ordeal. And that night, I killed her. Her legs seemed to me more beautiful than ever, jerking in the air, thrashing about this way and that as I suffocated her with my pillow until it was all over. Before the final trickle of life abandoned her body, I begged her to love me, in the darkness, from whatever well into which her soul might fall. Needless to say, I'd never have thought myself capable of such a thing. I harbored serious doubts as to my ability to see it through. I had to summon up the redskin I sometimes sense within me, I thought of white lambs, I thought of a cathedral filled with women and burning candles. Killing a human being is by no means easy, but sometimes there is nothing for it but to pluck up the courage and show some mettle. And, as they say around these parts, you can't learn how to castrate without chopping off a few balls.

20

(end)

One day the investigators will come, and they will know what I knew. They will know that Nadia was not innocent, nor did she really live in an apartment in which everything was white. They will perhaps find more cards, from other, previous, bunches of flowers, now rotten, decaying throughout the garbage dumps of the world. And in those words they will spot the clues to a game of love. One day the investigators will come, and they will know, just as I knew, that Nadia spent most nights with her husband in a house in Montecanal, from which she often escaped to redeem men, to caress brains trembling in fear. And they will know that I knew she was followed, night and day, by a few hired thugs who snapped her lovers' legs in two or left their faces scarred. They will discover that one day, at Jacobo's apartment, those thugs were met with resistance and that things got out of hand. No one expects, in the darkness of a hallway, in the middle of the night, to chance upon a madman defending himself brandishing an axe in both hands. They will search her little pampered wife's pad, the hideout for her mischief, the matching cushions and blinds. They will read the reports written up by the mercenaries, to be read by her husband while sitting in his office—what the eye sees through the semi-transparent curtains, the obscene poses struck by a couple of silhouettes, out-of-focus snapshots taken with a telephoto lens from the balcony across the street, recordings of moans behind doors, shot through with static but not so much so that he cannot make out, if he pricks up his ears, the echoes of a passion he has long forgotten and that cannot be rekindled except with the threat of a blade and the hounding of blood shivering invisibly in the air from the very first moment.

The investigators will turn up one day, and they will know that her husband loved her. And that he masturbated as he looked over the reports, observing those black smudges copulating behind the net curtains, shadows of flesh devouring each other. And that for her he risked jail, ruin, his whole life, only so that she might see how far, to what lengths. He would hold out his madness as proof of love and would make it up to her later with flowers and jewels whenever he broke a new toy of hers—here is my superhuman love, here are my wild eyes, my hands dirtied for you. The investigators will come, and it will take little effort for them to understand the dark pleasure Nadia took, in spite of herself and of her moments of doubt and of rage, in that game that could on no account be named, in that gift of danger galore, of pure intensity offered up to her on a plate for her days of tedium.

The investigators will turn up one day, and they will reach into the drawer containing her panties and hold them up to their noses when no one is looking. They will sniff the sheets, they will read every paper, and even when all of the evidence is staring them in the face, they will not wish to hear that she was a bitch or that she deserved to die. They will take with them only the fact that she was still young, poor thing, and that she leaves behind a teenage son and an unfinished woolen scarf she had been knitting for him. They will clutch at that so as to follow me over land and sea and hunt me down with their hounds.

My children will now be making their way home from school, their backpacks slung over their shoulders, at this hour as I write frantically, hiding out in a room in the Hôtel du Nord, once again, having checked in this time under my dead friend's name, a stone's throw from the Montparnasse cemetery where Duras's sorrow and the damp bones of a poet who died on a rain-sodden Thursday are reunited with the nothingness. It is not snowing today in Paris, nor are any cars burning on the outskirts of the city, and the Eiffel Tower stands as if rusting beneath a sky that is anything but picturesque.

I will never return to my apartment. A livid lady lies decomposing on my bed. I think of her greenish, splayed legs and of the maroon dress she was wearing. The investigators will find her there when the neighbors start to complain about the smell, or when one of the hired thugs, if indeed she was followed that last time, kicks the door down when she fails to show up. The investigators will turn up at my apartment, they will rifle through my things much as I have done these past months. They will look at the same things, they will see others. They won't even know what it is they're looking for among all those books, clippings, photos, and papers. They will throw everything to the floor, then trample it all underfoot. They will rummage around in the trash, in the medicine cabinet, touching everything with their clumsy paws.

One day the investigators will come, and perhaps one of them, at some point, will want to know the truth. Perhaps he will sit down in my battered leather wing chair to read the notes I wrote on Celan, the watercolor I commissioned from Jacobo of the poet from Czernowitz dropping into the Seine in the early morning, together with other prints from my collection of those who fell from the sky—Dorothy Hale, as seen by Frida Kahlo, her battered corpse on the asphalt next to Hampshire House, Evelyn McHale, fingering her necklace and yet immobile, dead atop the sunken roof of a limousine parked beneath the Empire State Building; he will perhaps discover my love for all those who took the plunge, those who leapt and those who fell—Hart Crane, Virginia Woolf, Primo Levi, so many others who took to the air on the darkest of nights, those who throw themselves into the sea, into the river, down the stairwell. He will be taken aback by so many photos of Auschwitz and bound women, of slaughterhouses for men and for cattle.

One day the investigators will come, and they will know that my life has been nothing. They will see that I have gone and that my things continue to float in the density of fear. It will dawn on them that many of the books remain unread. And that that raincoat-clad girl, her hair tied up, never came to browse my shelves. That no one came, and that that woman was not, therefore, as I had dreamt, the French girl who walked barefoot beneath the rain, holding her shoes in one hand. They will reach the conclusion that I sought to distance myself from it all without ever managing to find the doors to the empty cathedral inside which I was locked. They will learn that I screamed myself hoarse only to hear my own echo beneath the domes in reply. They will know that I gave in to the weariness, they will know that I did not know what to do with all my terror and also that I needed my friend's death in order to be able to see myself for the first time. One day the investigators will come, and they will learn of this darkness, of how desire and blood, silk and knives get caught up in the furrows of my brain. And they will see that I wanted to love but did not know how to, and that I wept for that reason, and that I aimlessly wandered the evenings of my life, mile after mile, without finding a thing, for there was nothing in the streets or the books or among the trees that was not tainted by the fear being secreted by my brain.

The investigators will turn up, and they will know that one night I paced up and down the Mirabeau Bridge, barefoot, beautiful, I think, without knowing what to do, without knowing if I might be found in a bend in the River Seine, bound for Le Havre, caught up in the reeds on the shore, or seated on a bed in a hotel room, with life in full flow, the TV on, my own tears, the bad light.

Cabo de Gata, August 2012

ABOUT THE AUTHOR

CARLOS CASTÁN is a Spanish writer born in Barcelona in 1960. He is considered one of the best short-story writers in Spain. *Bad Light* is his debut novel. He lives in Zaragoza.

ABOUT THE TRANSLATOR

MICHAEL MCDEVITT was a runner-up on the inaugural Harvill Secker/Granta Young Translators' Prize. He has translated work by Elvira Navarro, Agustín Fernández Mallo and Luisgé Martín, among others. His translations have been published by Two Lines Press, The White Review, Hispabooks and OpenRoad/Group Planeta. He lives in Madrid.

Lightning Source UK Ltd.
Milton Keynes UK
UKOW04f2327080216

267948UK00003B/99/P